Seen

THE LAGAN SERIES
SHAUNA ADAMS

Copyright © 2025 by Shauna Adams

All rights reserved.

No part of this book may be reproduced, distributed, or transmitted in any form or by any means, including photocopying, recording, or other electronic or mechanical methods, without the prior written permission from the author, except for the use of brief quotations in a book review.

This is a work of fiction. The story, names, characters, events and incidents portrayed in this work are fictitious. Any resemblance to actual persons, living or dead, or actual events is purely coincidental.

Without limiting the author's and publisher's exclusive rights, any unauthorised use of this publication to train generative artificial intelligence (AI) technologies is expressly prohibited.

All images used have been obtained with appropriate copyright by those involved in the production.

Cover Design: Juniper Hartmann
Internal imagery: Mark McStravick @Fujifella
Internal artwork: @Mynx
Editing and formatting by Jasmine Wallace of Demonic Publishing

Author's Note

'Seen' is book one in a series of standalone but interconnected stories. It is a dark and spicy romance containing content and situations that could be triggering for some readers.

This book is explicit and contains explicit sexual content.

It is intended for readers ages 18 years and over

Aodhan is waiting for you!

Shauna Adams

Trigger Warnings

Please read the following trigger warnings carefully:

Graphic Violence including death
Mutilation
Murder
Stalking
Obsessive Behaviours
Explicit Sexual Content
Drugs
Human Trafficking (off page)
Hidden camera
Home invasion
Swearing

Your mental health is important.

Dedication

This book is dedicated to all the dark romance girlies who love a morally grey fictional boyfriend but would kick his ass in real life.
Or would you?
Aodhán O'Neill is waiting for you...

Contents

1. Aodhán — 1
2. Aodhán — 9
3. Aodhán — 13
4. Nora — 22
5. Aodhán — 26
6. Nora — 29
7. Aodhán — 33
8. Nora — 40
9. Aodhán — 49
10. Nora — 56
11. Aodhán — 67
12. Nora — 72
13. Nora — 79

14.	Aodhán	82
15.	Nora	84
16.	Aodhán	89
17.	Nora	92
18.	Aodhán	95
19.	Nora	99
20.	Aodhán	103
21.	Nora	108
22.	Aodhán	113
23.	Nora	118
24.	Aodhán	122
25.	Nora	126
26.	Aodhán	130
27.	Nora	134
28.	Aodhán	136
29.	Nora	140
30.	Aodhán	144
31.	Nora	148
32.	Aodhán	153
33.	Nora	157
34.	Aodhán	162

35.	Nora	165
36.	Aodhán	168
37.	Nora	172
38.	Aodhán	176
39.	Nora	180
40.	Aodhán	184
41.	Nora	187
42.	Aodhán	191
43.	Nora	195
44.	Aodhán	199
45.	Aodhán	205
46.	Aodhán	209
47.	Cormac	213
48.	Riley	216
49.	Aodhán	219
50.	Nora	222
51.	Aodhán	225
52.	Nora	230
53.	Aodhán	234
54.	Nora	237
55.	Aodhán	242

56.	Nora	247
57.	Aodhán	251
58.	Nora	255
59.	Aodhán	259
60.	Nora	263
61.	Aodhán	267
62.	Nora	269
Glossary		275
Acknowledgements		277
About the author		279

Chapter One

Aodhán

Most people who know me will tell you I'm not a good man. I've committed some heinous and terrible things in my life, but I can honestly say that I was set up for this particular crime. This time I am completely innocent.

It is incomprehensive that someone could be so fucking stupid. I mean, who robs the local store with a balaclava and a crowbar while wearing gloves, then proceeds to batter the store owner to within an inch of his life, leaving him barely alive. Then, said person drops the crowbar around the corner from the store. Fucking amateurs, that's who. And what's worse, I'm in the frame for it.

The peelers have been trying to get me for years. They must have celebrated like all their Christmases came at once when my DNA showed up on the crowbar. I still don't know how that even happened, but I promise you one thing, I *will* get to the bottom of it.

It was infuriating that they wouldn't even listen to my fucking answers – but it doesn't matter. This time I have a rock-solid alibi, and it's actually legit. Although, the bastards wouldn't even confirm if they checked it out before taking me into custody.

Sad as it is, I never thought a speeding ticket would be my alibi, but I had no intention of telling them where I was going or why I was speeding in the first place. I'll happily take the ticket, and pay the fine, but I'll be fucking damned if I'm going down for aggravated burglary and assault.

I was on my way to one of our underground fights, some prick decided watching and gambling wasn't enough excitement for him, so he and his mates decided to take a run at my baby brother, Riley.

It's not like Riley can't handle himself–he *is* a prizefighter after all–or that the security team we had on-site couldn't have handled things just fine, but the crowd was drunk and fucking stupid, so they thought they'd join in and when it comes to my little brother, something animalistic, protective, takes over my mind and I couldn't wait to get there.

I should have been there in the first place, but no, I was balls deep in some piece of skirt. She wasn't even that good but she provided the distraction I was seeking. There really is just no thrill involved when these cheap and desperate women are falling all over themselves to get me into bed, but hey 'any hole's a goal' right? Anyway, when the call came in, I left her there without a second thought and raced over. The lads were handling it well enough and we got everything under control pretty swiftly, thankfully without any deaths this time.

Yes, you heard right. Just let me explain though. We had this one situation a load of months back when the punters got a little too carried away outside the ring. Some drunken dispute they were trying to settle with their fists. It seemed like it would be a waste to break it up, so we opened a book on it and let the others place bets. We made a fortune that night.

I guess we let it go too far. Against all the odds the scrawny little kid barely made it out alive while the other guy didn't make it at all. I suppose that's the risk you take when you start a scrap while attending an underground fight. It can get a bit messy but the clean-up afterwards was just not worth it in the end.

My family and I do what we need to survive, we didn't have much of a choice when the old man kicked the bucket five years ago and we were left with a pretty devastating choice of our own, step up to take the reins or allow that fucker, Murphy and his crew, to step in, and there was no chance they'd leave us alive if we did that.

There would always be a risk they would eventually come for our father's turf, so we did what we had to, and now we run most of West Belfast. We provide protection and security for the local bars and clubs.

We also run the local dealers selling drugs as a side project but I've always hated that side of things. Drugs were never my thing so I don't understand the attraction, not to mention the fact that it can be so messy, and there are far too many ways for the cops to wangle their way in.

Anyway, can you really believe it? A stupid fucking speeding ticket, turns out there was a new speed camera set up on the underpass at the Westlink, and going 80 miles an hour in a 50 limit gets you a fucking pricey picture.

Emmett O'Donoghue, my solicitor, is working on getting access to the speed camera records, which will prove I was getting my picture taken while that stupid twat was robbing the corner shop on the Whiterock and assaulting the owner. Perfect fucking alibi if only the lovely detectives had checked, but then again, they have no reason to want to clear me.

Once they check the records and the cameras, they will have to drop the charges against me, but until then I'm stuck in this shitshow, on remand, heading to my first appearance in court.

I hate this pokey wee hole they call a cell–it stinks of piss and shite. Despite my past indiscretions, I've always managed to avoid being in the back of one of these vans until now. Oh sure, a paddywagon, now that's a different story altogether. I've been lifted more times than I can remember, but they've never been able to make anything stick. I'm so scundered my first time isn't even one I can be proud of.

As I step out of the transport van–still handcuffed–I notice we are further back from the entrance. Overhearing the guards whispering, I learned that the previous van broke down inside the secure entry part of the car park so vans are lined up along the outer part of the building.

Descending down the steps I'm bundled towards the wall waiting for the others to decant. My eyelids close as I take a deep breath, enjoying the fresh air after being cooped up in that tin box. It makes me wonder if they ever clean them out.

Opening my eyes, I look around, taking in my surroundings, watching for any sign of weakness in security, checking for possible ways to capitalise on them and escape. Mentally preparing myself for if today doesn't go the way I expect, one way or another, I will get out of this bloody predicament. I'm not going to prison. Ultimately, I may very well belong there, but not for this. When I find the bastard that set me up, there will be hell to pay.

As I turn my head back to focus on the adjacent buildings, my whole world stands still as I see *her*.

She is stunningly beautiful and confidently strutting along the pathway, carefree, with her backpack slung over one shoulder and silently grinning–a phone in one hand, an extra-large coffee cup in the other.

Her curly blonde hair blowing in the breeze as she moves. Black trousers hugging her curves. A green v-neck top under a black blazer that just shows a hint of her voluptuous breasts. Those luscious lips are divine, her bottom lip now slightly caught between her teeth as she holds back a smile at whatever she is focusing on within the screen of her phone.

It's like time has frozen around me and all I can concentrate on is her. I've had my fair share of women but there is something about this one that has me completely intrigued. I can't put my finger on what it is but I want to know everything about her. I want to run my hands all over that body, kiss every inch of her skin and bury my head between those glorious breasts.

She has this air of confidence in the way she glides down towards the main building. Smiling and strutting like she hasn't a care in the world, *'dancing like no one is watching'* comes to mind. But I'm watching. I see her.

The prison officer shoves my shoulder, hurdling me forward and it pulls my attention away from her for just a second. Looking back in the direction of where she was, my eyes frantically search but find nothing. Just like that, she is gone.

The officer grunts, directing me inside the security gate and towards the custody suite. Perhaps this unfortunate predicament will be good for one thing. Her. Once I find a way to get myself out of this, I'm going to find her, and I am going to enjoy getting to know all about her.

As I sit in the holding cell, patiently waiting to make my appearance to the fuckers who think they have a chance of convicting me, I groan in frustration. It should never have gotten this far to begin with, but the peelers do love their fun. The noises here are so loud, grown men either screaming in anger or sobbing in despair. It is perhaps the most depressing place I have ever found myself. My mind drifts to trying to block it all out and she appears like a vision before my eyes. The curves, the breasts, those lips, how I would love to taste them.

Bang, bang, bang! The guard hits the door and drags me back to reality.

SEEN

It's showtime, walking up the steps towards the dock I motion to Emmett, he takes a step back and leans in with his brows furrowed into a look of concern. I issue two instructions – "Don't fuck this up mate, you need to get me fucking bail today and then I want a tech guy, top of the range skills. Whatever it costs and whatever it takes, I don't give a shit."

The second statement really throws him, his face full of confusion, but the stern look on mine, should tell him I'm not kidding. He doesn't need to know what I'm up to, he just needs to listen to my orders... and get it done.

Ten minutes later I am being hauled back to the custody cells to await transfer to prison. "Bail denied", "defendant is a flight risk" and "witness tampering is highly likely" are just a few statements I recall as the whole event is just a blur. What the fuck am I paying Emmett for? He botched that whole fucking thing. Getting bail shouldn't have been hard. I know they have DNA evidence, but I have an alibi! That should have counted for something.

I should be walking out the front door right now but I'm on my way to prison. Through my confusion and anger, she flits across my mind again. Nothing, and I mean nothing, not even the sham justice system is going to keep me from her.

Don't worry, little one, I'm coming for you.

My rage is getting hard to hold, my hands balled into fists, and my head feels like it's going to explode. I can't understand how Emmett fucked this up so badly... or did he? Is he in on this with the cops? Did he just betray me? My mind is racing a million miles an hour questioning everything.

I'm then escorted from the custody suite cells back to the prison transport, and my hopes of getting out of this are slipping away fast. The security around the place has really tightened up since we arrived this morning. I wonder if the broken van in the secure hold is the reason. Either way, there are twice as many cops guarding the place now and I can't see a way out.

Guess I'm just going to have to suck it up for now. and formulate a plan later. But there is no way I can stick this for the next 4 weeks until my next appearance.

Chapter Two

Aodhán

Mentally, it feels like I've been in this poxy cell a lot longer than 20 minutes. I shift in the seat, trying and failing to get comfortable, twitching like a crackhead searching for his next fix.

I start to slide, if that's what you could even call it, given that there is hardly any room for my size. This cell is smaller than the old-style phone boxes we used to have all over the place. It was subtle at first, the movement knocked me into the side wall, like the driver may have taken a corner too quickly.

Now it feels like the driver is swerving a lot, and I'm getting knocked from one wall to the other. What the fuck is going on?

The next thing I know, my body lifts out of the seat. If it wasn't for the neon yellow seat belt holding me in place, I would have been tossed around this box like a pinball. The van feels like it's rolling as gravity takes over. Either we hit something, or something really big hit us.

Finally, we come to a stop, and my body aches all over. Thankfully, I don't think anything is broken, but I will definitely feel the whiplash in the morning. The soft blue lights in the cell have gone out, and I can't see a thing when I look through the tiny window on the van door. I strain to listen, trying to see if I can hear what's going on, but all I can hear are screams and groans from the other prisoners.

A sliver of white light appears, but I still can't make out what is happening. Then I hear it, a sound I'm all too familiar with. The distinct noise of an angle grinder, the loud whirl of the blades scratching loudly as they bite through the metal becomes deafening. I just about see the sparks fly before I lean against the back wall of my cell, trying to formulate a plan that is completely eluding me right now. Shite is about to get really fucked up; this was no accident. It's a fucking direct hit.

I hear the cell doors being wrenched open one by one. It sounds like whoever this is, they are looking for someone specifically. I try looking out through the tiny window in the cell door again, but I can't make anything out in the dark. The sliver of light appears to be moving along with the noise like a torch searching for their target. I wish I wasn't handcuffed. I feel so defenceless right now. I hope this isn't a hit on me because I'm a goner if it is, there is no room in this suffocating cell to even allow me to gain some leverage for whatever comes through that door. This is not how my life is supposed to end.

The noises are getting closer, my breathing is hurried, my heart is racing, but then I hear my brother Cormac's voice.

"I bet the fucker is in the last one. It's always the last fucking one," he laughs as he opens my cell door. Relief washes over me. *Thank fuck*, is the first thing that crosses my mind, but then the confusion kicks in. What the hell is going on?

He takes a quick look back, as if he is checking for something before turning to me with that stupid smirk on his face. "Let's go, little brother, we don't have a lot of time. Those fuckers got a distress signal out before you crashed" I follow him out, still completely confused as to what the hell is going on. I look around and see the carnage, the escorting officer is unconscious by the front steps, the transport van is battered, and there is a forty-footer with a busted front grill just back a bit on the main road.

"Mac, did you seriously take the prison van out with a lorry?" I laugh, still trying to discern what is going on.

"Yup, now come on we gotta get out of here" he laughs. He motions to the black Range Rover parked nearby and ushers me into the backseat. Riley swings around from the driver's seat., "Welcome back to freedom," he says with a cheeky grin.

Before I can even get stuck into Emmett, who is sitting in the front passenger side, asks Cormac, "Did you let everyone else out too?"

"I did. Having them all on the run diverts resources from this one," Mac replies as he slaps me on the back before adding, "All except that shitehawk Dargan. He was up on rape charges this morning, and this was not his first rodeo, so I stuck a bullet in his head, plus it will keep the peelers guessing too."

Cormac is a tough guy, someone I've always looked up to. Then again, I suppose most men look up to their older brothers. He scares me sometimes, and he clearly drives the fear of God into everyone else he meets. He might be rough around the edges, but there's one thing he won't tolerate... rapists. He has a true respect for women and woe betide anyone who harms one.

I turn my attention to Emmett, who sits with a stupid fucking grin on his face. "You may start explaining yourself and do it quickly, or you'll end up like Dargan."

He sniggers, "Now, now, there is no need for that. We figured you'd prefer to do what you like with that tech guy without having to stick to strict bail restrictions. We can run interference, providing you aren't doing anything stupid."

The tension in my face eases. I knew he was curious about my second instruction. I just never thought he'd take this route, and my mind boggles as to how they pulled it off in such a short time frame. But right now I don't care enough to ask. They have no idea what I'm planning, nor do I plan on sharing, but I like the way Emmett's thinking. Perhaps he's smarter than I give him credit for.

As the engine roars and we pull away from the destruction left behind, a thought occurs to me. "Emmett, speaking of tech guys, there were cameras all over that van, even inside each cell. Might be worth getting yer man on that too. Just in case, ya know."

Cormac leans in and grips my shoulder. "No need. I swiped the disc from the recorder."

Chapter Three

Aodhán

Oscar, the tech guy Emmett set me up with, managed to confirm within seconds that the van footage wasn't transmitting anywhere. Mac had already told me as much, but better safe than sorry as the saying goes.

Once he completed that little task, he set about trawling footage for me, and he has now been trying to track her for days. He's a strange little man. Then again, most men are little compared to me. I am 6'1", built like a brick shitehouse, as they would say. It comes in handy when dealing with rowdies in the clubs or at the Underground fights.

I've been watching him for hours, trying to work out who he reminds me of, and it literally just hit me this minute. The little hacker dude from that film 'The Core'. He looks just like him, a skinny little nerd with floppy brown hair and an open shirt with some weird design that is draped over a t-shirt. It's uncanny. Even down to the way he is munching away as he types. Albeit,

Oscar has sausage rolls instead of hot pockets but still. He's been stuck behind that laptop, combing through security footage in the surrounding buildings, with no luck so far.

I'm starting to think she was just a figment of my imagination. I can't give up, though. I need to find her. She's become an obsession I can't quite shake, and the sensation of it... is irritating as fuck. It's the strangest of feelings. A few seconds was all I had, but it was all I needed to know. She was special, and something about her just felt like home.

I got tired of waiting around while Oscar kept striking out. So, despite the obvious bad reasons, I've been staking out the coffee shop across from the courthouse for the last week, hoping to spot her. I remembered the style of the cup she was holding. The trademark green symbol wasn't hard to miss. Doubt begins to creep in, though. Maybe I did imagine her, like a mirage in the desert when you are dying of thirst.

Doubt or not, I find myself, yet again, sitting at a table by the window with another black coffee, trying to be inconspicuous, while also not looking like someone trying to hide. Although perhaps I'm thinking too hard. I mean, lots of guys sit in coffee shops in Jeans, with a hoodie and a baseball cap pulled down to try to hide their faces. Right?

I've been here for almost two hours. Maybe it's time to give up for the day. Maybe tomorrow will be the one. Perhaps she only works on certain days or was only there for that one day. Who'd have thought trying to track down a girl you saw for just a few seconds would be so difficult?

I'm not giving up. I can't. I'm determined to find her, even if at this stage, just to satisfy myself that I didn't make her up. Surely, my imagination can't be that good, can it?

As I drink the last of my coffee and motion to stand, I catch a glimpse of a curvy blonde woman coming up the steps outside. My mind is running rampant. Could this actually be her? Is it possible I'm not crazy? Have I found her after all?

My heart races. She takes each step with her head down, staring into her phone. I silently beg for her to look up. She eventually does as she reaches the top step. Sweet fuck, it *is* her. I collapse back into my seat and watch as she comes through the door effortlessly, straight to the counter, and orders her coffee.

From where I'm sitting across the room, I can't hear her voice like I desperately want to. Willing my legs to move, I finally stand and move towards the counter to be closer to her, right between her and the door, and I silently watch her flick through her phone, oblivious to the world around her. Oblivious to me watching her every move. She is even more beautiful than the image I've been carrying around in my head. She mesmerises me all over again.

"Nora," the barista calls out, and she steps forward to grab her coffee.

"Thanks, Nick. Have a lovely day," she replies with that beautiful smile. I want to gouge his eyes out for even looking at her, never mind that fucking grin on his face as she turns to leave. Why does she even know his name? I move closer to the door and reach out to open it as she walks closer towards me.

I hold the door open, and as she passes by me to leave, I lean in ever so slightly and close my eyes. I inhale a breath. Fuck, she smells so good. Somehow, from that first moment that I saw her, I just knew she would. I want to grab her and taste her right now, but I need to bide my time. I can't afford to mess this up. Not with her. And because I'm supposed to be keeping a low profile.

"Thanks," she says without even looking up in my direction. Her voice is as intoxicating as her scent. It was only a single word, but I can't wait to hear my name in that beautiful sound.

Her focus is completely on her phone as she walks towards the road. I carefully follow behind, pulling my cap down further to hide my face but never taking my eyes off her.

Nora, my réaltín álainn, is real and right in front of me. I can hardly breathe as I watch her walk along the pavement with that same confident nonchalant strut as the first time I saw her.

She stands for a few minutes, looking back and forth along the road, waiting for the traffic to ease before crossing. She lifts her hand and waves towards the security dome. She stands for a moment, and when the gate opens, she disappears inside.

Yup, I'm totally fucked now. She's real, and I can't and won't stop until she's mine.

SEEN

The nationwide manhunt is well underway for me and the other six guys who were in my prison transport, and so far, after almost a week, they haven't been able to recapture any of us. Thanks to the lack of footage from inside the van, they haven't been able to work out if the crash was an escape attempt and Dargan was unlucky or if it was a planned hit on him, and the rest of us took advantage and ran.

That's good news for me. The longer it takes the cops to decipher what happened and round up the rest of the escapees, the fewer resources they will have centred specifically on me. I'm supposed to be hiding out while Emmett works on getting the evidence to clear my name, then find a way to hand myself in without getting new charges added. But now I've found the blonde goddess, I just can't seem to get her off my mind or stay away from her.

Cormac continues to work on finding out who the fuck set me up. My money is still on that bastard Murphy or someone in his crew. He's hated my family for years, and it's just like him to pull this kind of bullshit

I'm sure Emmett will figure something out. I know I underestimated him before, but I trust he will get this sorted. For now, I guess my only concern is trying to get enough information on Nora for Oscar to track down everything I need to know.

Now that I know I didn't imagine her, I want to know every little thing about her. It may be a long shot but I'm hoping that given that she came up from the lower levels of Victoria

Square towards the coffee shop, she uses the car park there. That means I'm going to have to hang around here and wait for her to hopefully come back this way.

As I watch her leave the same car park I first saw her in last week, I marvel once again at her beauty. Those curves in all the right places, breasts I would gladly be smothered in, and an ass I could just grab for days.

Her blonde hair, which framed her face this morning, is now scooped up in a ponytail, and I wish I could get closer to inhale her sweet smell, something similar to lavender and bergamot. But she glides past me, out of reach with her head down. *Turn around, baby show me that pretty face.* Much to my annoyance, she continues walking, never looking back.

I step forward from the wall I've been leaning on to follow her. She is so lost in her phone oblivious yet again to everything around her.

Is she usually this ignorant of her surroundings?

Christ, if I was a lesser man, I could easily take advantage of her without even being caught. Not that anything is likely to happen to her, not now I have my eyes on her.. I would gladly beat the granny out of anyone who even tried to lay a finger on her pretty little head. She may not know it yet, but she is mine, and no one touches what is mine.

She danders down the main steps to the ground floor of Victoria Square and then continues down the escalators into the underground car park. Yes! I was right; she does park there. This is undeniably good news for me.

Oscar mentioned that he could access the car and licensing database as well as the traffic cams, so I just need to find out her car registration, and he can do the rest. Smiling to myself, I slow my pace down, just slightly, though. I don't want to bring attention to myself down here where there are fewer people. I can't risk her being spooked, either.

As she reaches her car, I can't help but grin. It's so her—a sleek little black number. She throws her backpack in the boot before climbing into the car. Hiding behind one of the pillars, I get just close enough to take a picture of the car and the number plate.

And just like that, it's sent through to Oscar as I watch her drive away. She has the windows down and music is blaring like she doesn't have a care in the world. Like her world isn't about to completely change. Hopefully, this will be enough for him to work out who she is.

Take care, little one. I'll see you real soon.

It really didn't take Oscar long to trace her details once he had the number plate. Her full name is Eleanora Kavanagh. Thinking back to the coffee shop I remember her stepping forward when the barista called the name Nora. She obviously prefers to be called Nora. It unequivocally suits her better. I'd prefer her to be called *Mine*, but we will get there.

Armed with her address, I find myself unable to keep away, and leaving Oscar's place, I head straight there. Her apartment is on the second floor, which means it's not as easy to spy in. I thought about a drone, but they are noisy wee bastards. I'll have to think about something else. I hung around for a couple of hours, hoping to catch a glimpse of her or hoping she'd have to nip out for something, anything. Unfortunately for me, she didn't, so when the lights went out around midnight, I headed back to the safe house.

The next morning, as she ducks into the coffee shop, I'm right behind her. This time, I hear her voice as she orders her ridiculously long coffee order, and when the girl behind the counter asks her if she wants whipped cream, I miss her response.

My mind wandered, thinking about what I'd do with whipped cream if I had her alone. I've never been one for using food in a sexual way or doing any kind of sex play of any sort, but I find myself imagining all the things I would like to do to that curvaceous body in front of me. I feel myself getting hard at the thought of it all.

Adjusting myself, I take a step closer so that when she turns to leave the counter, she bangs right into me. Her phone and her bag fall to the ground. She is flustered and quickly crouches to grab her things off the floor. Damn, she looks so good on her knees.

Her head lifts, and her eyes meet mine as she attempts to apologise, but she stops for a second and stares at me through those luscious locks. I'm entranced by the sparkle of her sapphire blue eyes as she takes my breath away, not for the first time.

"I'm sorry. I wasn't watching where I was going, but seriously mate, ever heard of personal space," she scoffs as I offer my hand to gently aid her back to her feet.

"Of course, it's no bother, réaltín álainn." I watch as her cheeks blush with a hint of rosy pink as she struggles to think about what to say next. She grabs her things in a hurried manner, keeping her head down and her face out of my eyeline as she avoids any further contact, then rushes to the door before I can say anything else.

Chapter Four

Nora

What the fuck was that? My chest constricts as I struggle to catch my breath. I wasn't going to stop for my usual order of coffee this morning but back-to-back meetings with senior management required an extra caffeine kick. I can't believe I just barrelled into that guy like such an idiot. God knows what he thought. Although, I mean, he was standing so close, what did he expect?

Well, I can tell you what I didn't expect, pure unadulterated sex on legs, and those were some pretty long legs. But it was that manly smell that did the real damage to my mind, had I not already been nearly on the floor, it would have had me down there in a puddle.

It invaded my nose, boring a hole, and imprinting on my brain. It was something woody with a hint of spiciness and oh man, that body, all hard and muscular with a tattoo peeking out of his collar, he looked like one of my favourite authors wrote him.

Chestnut brown hair with flecks of caramel peaked out from below the seam of the hoodie framing his face. Smouldering blue eyes, brimming with an intensity that drills straight through your soul. His cheeks and jaw so chiseled I'm sure I would cut myself on them. And that thick luscious beard that I just want to trail my fingers through, dragging his lips to mine.

I bolt out of the shop, coffee in hand and rush towards the crossing, my heart going like the clappers. I just have to make it through the security gate and then I can relax.

Shit! Unless he's a member of staff.

My mind races and my heart beat rises, panic showing no signs of abating. No, I begin to convince myself, surely I'd have seen him about the building. There was no way I could have missed someone who looked like him. Plus I didn't see a lanyard or a backpack, or so I tried to reason with the panic attack nipping at the surface of my resolve.

The introduction of hybrid working and office transformation means we all carry backpacks now as we lug our laptops in and out of work for the days we work from home. Nope, I definitely didn't notice a laptop bag. I continue to try and convince myself as I walk through the security gate.

It's going to be a long fucking day. How am I supposed to concentrate after this? My mind continuously replayed those few seconds; the feel of his body, the delicious sound of his voice, and that intoxicating smell.

Yes, it's going to be a very long day indeed.

Meeting after meeting and yet somehow, I managed to make it through the day uneventfully. Packing up to leave the office for the day, I decide despite the disaster of a visit this morning, I'm going to stop to grab a coffee for the drive home—rush hour is always a nightmare. Hopefully, this caffeine visit will be a lot more straightforward than previously. I mean it can't be much worse, right? I clear the security gate with a quick wave to the guard who opens it up.

I stand on the edge of the pavement waiting for the traffic to stop just enough so I can shoot across the road, which feels like forever at this time of day. People are so keen to get home they block the crossings and then move forward so it never feels like there's a break in traffic. Guess I'm not getting away that easily tonight.

Looking back down the street I see the line of cars, trucks and buses moving at a continual snail's pace. My phone pings as I get a message, well a calendar notification that the new Georgia C Leigh book, 'Beast', I've signed up for is due in my inbox in the next hour. It's the latest in my paranormal romance phase, who doesn't like the idea of demons and angels right?

"That's my evening sorted." I smile excitedly to myself. After a long day of meetings, demands on my attention for decisions

SEEN

or advice, and the constant chittering of bullshit, I need a break. And the only thing I'm interested in right now, is a nice soak in the bath and a relaxing night at home with demons and angels at my fingertips.

Chapter Five

Aodhán

I really need to be careful being this close to the courthouse and the bloody police station next door. But hey, fortune favours the brave. And my réaltín álainn is here. Having spent most of the day hiding out in the back of the coffee shop, reading through the file that Oscar had composed for me, I already feel like I know her a lot better.

According to her social media accounts, she is single and has been for a while.

Well, there's one less complication here.

Not that it wouldn't have been easy to get around someone else in the picture, but now that I've found her, I'm not letting anyone else get in the way of what I want.

She's also an avid reader, mostly romance novels, and judging by the reviews on some of these, I'm not sure romance is the correct term. There is some seriously fucking dark shite going on in some of these books. I'm not sure I even want to know why some of the reviews state that cookies and cream ice cream is now off the menu. Perhaps I'll pick up a few of the ones she's read already, it wouldn't hurt to understand exactly what she likes, and it might even just give me some ideas.

I watch as she crosses the road. This is my chance. She walks towards me, head lost in that phone of hers, again with that beautiful grin of hers. Those beautiful juicy lips curved upward begging to be kissed, claimed. They look so soft and inviting. I can't help but stare, thinking how much I would love to just grab her, shove her up against the wall and crush my own into them. Too soon, all in good time.

Just as she approaches me, I step forward and directly into her path, too late for her to avoid me and she crashes straight into me. She stumbles but remains on her feet this time, while her phone hits the ground.

"Twice in one day, you stalking me, darlin'?" I sigh playfully, trying desperately to hide my delight.

Shocked and horrified she looks up and I see a blush fill her beautiful face. Just like it did this morning. Her cheeks are now filled with an enticing, dusted hue of pink that flows all the way down her throat to her chest.

"I... ah seriously. You... again? And no, I'm not stalking you. Big headed much."

Ooh, snappy.

She splutters trying to compose herself, clearly affected by me as much as I'm affected by her. Well, here's to hoping anyway.

"I'm sorry I wasn't looking where I was going, this time," she says with a barb, clearly implying—and quite rightly so that this morning was my fault. Although to be fair, she isn't aware that both times are wholly my fault. "Are you ok?" she says rather sheepishly this time.

"Me, yes, I'm fine, but perhaps you need to watch where you are walking," I reply, trying hopelessly to maintain an air of innocence. What a joke right? There is nothing innocent about any of this. I stifle a laugh as I try to regain my own composure. "What's so interesting about that phone anyway?" She eyes me suspiciously and I laugh, "Ok, ok, I'm only kidding but why don't you let me buy you a coffee, to properly apologise for this morning."

I watch her ponder for just a second as it seems like she is considering my offer, and then she shakes her head.

"No thanks, not interested," she quips, before strutting off like only she can; with a flick of her hair, and leaving me standing there like a fucking moron. Never in my life have I been turned down by a woman as quickly as she just did.

I'd have happily taken her for coffee and started from there, but this is better. I like it. Experiencing the thrill of the chase for the first time in my life, sends a shot of electricity up my spine, and a smirk on my face I can't stop.

I smile as I watch her walk away and laugh to myself. She has no idea what is coming.

Chapter Six

Nora

I really need to watch where I'm going for fucks sake. I rush down the steps to the car park and hurry to my car, dramatically hoping he's not following me. My face is still beaming as I fumble with my ticket, trying desperately to get away from here as fast as I can.

Sitting at the traffic lights I can feel the embarrassment wash over me as I replay the whole interaction with the hot mystery man. I kind of wish I'd said yes to that coffee, because in all the bloody commotion… I didn't even get one myself. I don't even know his name but that deep throaty accent chilled me right to my core. And, oh man, his scent—spicy with a hint of musk—had me wondering what it would feel like encapsulating me on a bed of Egyptian cotton bed sheets. Frowning, mentally kicking myself, why didn't I just say yes?

Thankfully the traffic wasn't too bad, then again, once I pumped the music up so loud the bass was vibrating through the seats—making me feel very beat to the point of making me dance in my seat—time just slipped away and I made it home in no time at all. Gathering my belongings together, I drag them and myself into my building, and up the stairs to my apartment.

Fumbling through my handbag, I finally locate my keys and drudge inside. I drop my bags on the side board just inside the door and grab a few pouches of cat food from the kitchen to feed my little furballs, Sooty and Ghost. The little rascals were hovering and meowing like they had been starved for days when I came in. They twirl themselves in and around my legs as I fill their bowls, purring loudly while they munch through the food as I quietly walk away.

Entering the kitchen, I pull the largest wine glass I own and grab the wine I left to chill in the fridge, pouring myself a glass before then heading to the bathroom to run a bath. There is nothing in the world quite like a long hot soak in a bubble bath to wash away the day's troubles.

I've always been the type of reader who gets completely submerged into a book and can picture the scenes like a movie playing in my head, mostly with me as the female lead. Normally, I try to picture the male characters by the descriptions, and match them to the closest actor it resembles. Or I just pick one I think encompasses the personality described. But tonight, my imagination is veering very specifically towards the mystery man I bumped into twice today.

Lying back in the bath, my eyes fall closed, and all I can see are his thick arms covered in tattoos. His strong calloused hands running all over my body. The memory of how he smelt when I crashed into him this morning has me feeling very horny. A raging heat begins to build and I trace my fingers over my breasts imagining it's his fingers. I pinch my nipples before gliding my hand down my body and in between my legs. A moan escapes as I imagine the feel of him all around me.

My imagination kicks into overdrive and I can almost feel him leaning in to kiss me in an all-consuming, bruising kind of kiss, with his hands firmly holding my head in place while his thumbs massage my cheeks. His lips move down the column of my throat, and along my collarbone. Taking a nipple in his mouth, sucking, and then a sharp bite before moving slowly along my stomach, placing his head between my legs and lapping at my core.

I mimic the motions with my fingers, inserting two fingers in and out of my pussy while circling my clit with my thumb. All while imagining him between my legs. I can feel my orgasm starting to build, and while my other hand is gripping my breast, I hook my fingers up to add pressure to my g spot. My breathing becomes ragged, the pressure enough to push me over the edge as my orgasm comes crashing over me leaving me breathless and shuddering in place.

As the sensations begin to subside, I sink further into the bath and begin to giggle a little. I can't believe I just came thinking about a complete stranger, who's name I don't even know.

Chapter Seven

Aodhán

I followed her home last night and watched as she entered her apartment block. It's been a fly in the ointment in terms of being able to watch her, but it won't be for long. I can't wait to take her home. To *our* home.

I sat in my car outside her building for hours just watching her window, hoping for a glimpse of her, which I briefly got when she closed the curtains as darkness began to fall. I began thinking about our interaction today and those luscious lips and feisty attitude got me a little hot and bothered, until my phone rang and interrupted a perfectly good daydream.

Emmett and Oscar finally got the camera footage from my speeding ticket. I'm surprised, given Oscar's skills, that it has taken this long, but I suppose at least now we have it. I have to admit though it's a rather good picture of me, even if I do say so myself. And what's even better, it is time stamped to exactly when I was supposed to be on the Whiterock, robbing that shop and beating the owner.

There is no way the peelers can continue to dispute my alibi now. They have to accept they were wrong and drop the charges. Emmett even has a plan on how we get away with the escape. It's a stretch in my opinion, but hey he's confident, and I've learned my lesson when it comes to doubting him.

I've spent all morning couped up in a tiny interview room within the Major Crime Suite at Musgrave Police Station, which just so happens to be located right next door to the courthouse where my feisty réaltín álainn works. This is certainly not a place I would normally choose to spend my time but this needed sorting.

Emmett's been raising all bloody hell on how the charges for the assault and robbery needed to be quashed now that we have concrete evidence showing it couldn't have been me. It's actually been quite impressive watching him work. Usually he's trying to get me out of a scrape I put myself in with my line of work, which can be dodgy.

The detectives were a little shocked to say the least, that we obtained the footage of my speeding infringement, but there was no disputing it. Especially when the sergeant actually checked the validity of it this time. Then came the questioning on the escape and where I'd been for the past week or so. Was I involved? Do I know who killed Dargan? Was he the primary target? It went on for hours.

Emmett had me well-prepped. We'd spent most of the night going over the story, so I knew it backward, to the point where I almost started to believe it. I'd been in hiding. No, there was no one else involved in hiding me. Obviously I wasn't going to implicate anyone else in this palava. I told them the place I was hiding out in was an abandoned house in Lisburn, only reaching out to my solicitor the night before. I told them about hearing the noise from the angle grinder and I heard how 'they' went from cell to cell. It was important to make out like there were two considering my cell was across from Dargan's and further up.

Only one assailant would throw my story into jeopardy. Cormac had ensured no one else saw his face, and considering the gunshot went off before he found me, if anyone remembered his words, they would attribute them to someone looking for Dargan. Emmett's story centred on ensuring that his murder was the motive for the hit and our escape—or mine in particular, was one of circumstance.

They put me through the wringer during those hours, trying to get me to slip up on the details, so much so it actually felt like I'd gone 12 rounds with Riley, and that kid hits hard. I've never been so impressed with Emmett's prep. He went at me for hours last night, drilling me over every single detail until I got it perfect. Neither these detectives, nor the sergeant who joined us later, were able to rattle me, not one single iota.

After recounting the story for the umpteenth time, Emmett finally asked for a break. I knew at that point we were on the home stretch. He warned me the night before, that when he asked for a break, it was the signal that we were done. He was taking things up a gear, they'd had their chance to expose any weakness in my story now it was time to shut this shite down for good. After 10 minutes, the officers stepped back in, and before they could resume their inquisition, Emmett demanded that I be released immediately without any further charges. That took them a little by surprise.

Given the complete fuck up on the original arrest, Emmett said if any further charges were brought concerning the escape and crash, he'd have them all up on wrongful arrest and prosecutorial misconduct. My story about the crash held up for all intents and purposes, so it didn't take long for the Public Prosecution Service to drop everything and I was, once again, a free man.

Walking towards the exit, I thank Emmett for all his hard work. No matter what, that man always has my back. Moving closer to the main exit, Emmett turnsback to say something that I never quite caught, due to seeing Nora walking passed with two other women. I briefly stepped behind Emmett so she wouldn't notice me, then as she moves out of sight, I step out of the gate and onto the street.

SEEN

"Thanks again big man for getting me sorted, I really appreciate it. Listen, I'm good from here, I'm going to make my own way back. Tell Cormac we need to get moving on the opening now that I'm in the clear," I almost shout to Emmett as I head off in her direction. I don't even wait for a response.

I follow behind, far enough that I'm not right behind them, but close enough I can just about make out the conversation. They chat about work, and their plans for the weekend. The little redhead has plans with her husband and the woman with the dark blonde hair is heading out with friends, but my little blonde goddess is planning on curling up with a good book and bottle of wine.

That's not good. If she's at home all weekend, how am I going to see her? As I contemplate the next few days camped outside her apartment block, a deviously brilliant idea hits me just as we round the corner towards Custom House Square. I take my phone out and flick through my contacts to call Oscar.

"Alright big lad, how's it going?" he groans once he finally answers.

"Grand, Emmett just got everything straightened out so I'm in the clear, this time. But listen, I need a favour."

"What can I do you for?" he replies.

"I need some discreet cameras, preferably ones that can pick up sound, and I need them today."

He's silent for a moment before confirming he has what I need and asks for the address. "No need mate I'll just pick them and sort that part myself." I don't want him or anyone else anywhere near her place.

"No bother, they'll be here waiting on you," he laughs, and I hang up, feeling a little excited and pretty darn content with my own ingenuity.

As I follow Nora and the two women, they continue on their walk, right past the front of the courthouse and down toward the market. It occurs to me that I haven't been there for years. Walking in through the doors on the left hand side, it's exactly how I remember it. Fish stalls at the front, butchers and fruit stalls in the middle, hot food down towards the back and along the right-hand side, stalls laden with buns and cakes down the left side.

Nora and the other two women wander in and out of the aisles and then stop at one of the hot food counters. I watch her receive what looks like a full Belfast Bap. My réaltín álainn has good taste. There is nothing better than a woman who likes her grub. Once they pick up some cream buns they head for the exit and I step forward trying to get a better view of my girl, but I notice Nora turning in my direction and I duck down behind the fruit stall. I made that joke yesterday about her stalking me and whilst, yes, I get the irony of it, I'm not ready to give this up just yet. I'm having fun watching her, for now.

By the time I look up again, she is gone. I take out my phone and call Riley. "Right wee man, I need to be picked up, I'm outside George's Market".

He laughs and replies, "We were wondering where you'd fled to after the peelers let you go."

"Just a wee dander round the block." I shake my head and laugh, "So are you lifting me or what? I just need to be dropped to my car.'"

"Aye I'm on the way," he says, and I step outside onto the street to wait.

Half an hour and dozens of questions later, Riley drops me off to pick up my car and I head straight to Oscar's to pick up the cameras.

Chapter Eight

Nora

Friday isn't normally a day I work in the office but with one of our cases due to close, here I am. My team and I spent all morning putting the finishing touches to it before it was ready to be released. Dealing with requests for information is interesting but some of these requestors are just nuts. There are days I curse the introduction of free access to all personal data.

The one upshot to working in the office on a Friday, is that it coincides with a day that St George's Market is running. It boasts the most amazing food stalls and is the perfect place for lunch.

Clara, Melissa, and I usually go for a lunchtime walk to get in those all-important steps, and today is no different as we head out the back of the courthouse, up Victoria Street, and round past the Big Fish, before hitting up the market to pick up some lunch and afternoon treats to bring back to the office.

SEEN

Walking into the market, I am amazed as always by the smells. Fresh fish stalls line the front wall as you walk in, and it smells like the beach. Salty and fresh. Stalls filled with the freshest prawns, scallops, white fish, and—the best type in my opinion—smoked fish. Those yellow-tinged fillets remind me of Friday nights at home with my parents, smoked fish, mashed potatoes, petit pois and that deliciously smoked white sauce my mum always made.

The memory hits me like a freight train and a pang of sadness wells up inside me, I miss my folks. It's been 10 years, and their death still weighs heavy on my heart. Don't get me wrong, I was an adult when they died, but with no other family I was all on my own. Looking back, I would have really struggled if not for my two best friends. They got me through some real tough days when I didn't think I would even survive the grief.

Anyway, across from the fish stalls, there are tables covered in fresh fruit and vegetables, butcher stands with scores of options, all sorts of steaks, chicken, and then the different types of sausages, beef and black pudding, pork and dulse, to the wacky pork, apple, and white chocolate. I tried them once, but I wouldn't recommend them really.

Moving further towards the centre of the market are the bakery stalls, sporting the most amazing-smelling treats. Raspberry and blueberry scones as big as your head, the famous Guinness and Wheaten loaf, as well as the fanciest of pastry tarts.

Walking towards the back of the market we see the hot food stalls. There are so many options to choose from. Falafel Extraordinaire, Crepes to go, Belfast Bap Burgers, Mexican Burritos, Paella Bella and so many more. I want to try everything, but I finally settled on a filled Belfast Bap. I mean it would be rude not to, right?

Nothing beats a sausage, bacon, and egg Belfast bap for lunch, so that's what's on the menu today for me. Melissa grabs a cheeseburger, while our resident veggie, Clara, opts for a baked potato with cheese and beans.

With lunch secured we meet in the middle of the market and move towards the bakery stall for some amazing fresh cream and jam buns. Those always go so nicely with a coffee in the afternoon, and then we make our way back towards the exit ready to walk back to the office.

As we motion closer to the outside, I spot a stall with, get this, Rocket Fuel Coffee. *The strongest coffee in existence*, or so the sign reads, and I can't help but take that challenge. Waiting for my order to be fulfilled, I turn around taking one last look around the market.

Remembering the old days before the pandemic, when I came here every week, the sights, the sounds are all so familiar and yet a little muted now. Scanning back towards the stall in front me, something catches my eye. I thought I noticed a man off to the left. But as I turn back to look in that direction, there is no one there.

"Everything ok?" Clara asks as she notices my sudden stop and turn.

SEEN

"Erm... yeah, I just thought I saw someone.. I must have imagined it," I reply, still trying to work out if I'm trying to convince her or myself.

"Seriously Nora, you need to stop reading all those dark romance novels, you'll give yourself nightmares," Melissa jokes.

I shake off the feeling lying deep in my gut and we leave through the main entrance at the front. Walking back to the office, I can't help but look around with more purpose than before. The feeling of being watched continues to build until we reach the staff entrance and only then does it dissipate.

The rest of the day passes without incident, and I am running for the door as 4 pm hits. It's Friday and I am ready to start enjoying my weekend. My fridge is packed with food and wine and my growing 'to be read' pile of books is mapped out for maximum reading sprints. The traffic on a Friday is so light that it takes no time at all to get home thankfully.

Within minutes of being at home, I am in my comfy clothes and ready to relax. Just as I pour myself a large glass of wine–because who pours small ones–my phone pings.

> **Emily:**
> Right ladies, I've had a nightmare of a week and I need my girlies, cocktails and dancing til the sun comes up.

> **Jenna:**
> Ok, but I'm not getting all dressed up. Where are we going?

> **Me:**
> I've literally just poured a glass of wine and got into my comfies. Please don't make me change.

> **Emily:**
> Don't make me drag you out. Come on. It will be fun. I PROMISE!!

> **Jenna:**
> I'm getting ready now. Nora, get your ass up and dressed.

> **Me:**
> Fiiiine! I'm in. See you bitches soon xx

An hour later I dressed in my tight black jeans, cowboy boots, and my favourite low-cut shirt. I'm a curvy girl–overweight my doctor calls it–but no matter what diet or exercise I try I can't seem to lose weight. I love my food and as much as I get self-conscious at times, I'm at the stage now where I just don't care anymore.

We hit the local club and several shots in, I've got my buzz on. Dance floor here I come. After dancing, and a fair amount of alcohol, I'm relaxing just as Rihanna's 'S&M' comes over the speakers. Sexy moves are engaged and I'm loving life, that is, until some random guy starts leering all over me.

His hands latch on to my hips and his body presses up against mine as he tries to dance along with me. Rolling my shoulder, I attempt to wriggle out of his grip but he doesn't take the hint.

"Seriously mate, take a hike. I'm not interested." I try to shrug his hands off me as I turn to face him.

"Ah, come on baby, I could show you a good time." His knuckles graze my cheeks and it repulses me.

"In your dreams." I turn away from him and try to ignore him as I continue to dance.

He grabs my waist and whispers into my ear, "If you want, sweetheart." My whole body shivers and goosebumps begin to form, not in a good way.

"Don't fucking call me 'sweetheart', arsehole." I shove him back and walk off the dance floor, heading for the bar leaving him standing there.

"Thought you were on the hunt for a man tonight," Jenna laughs as I approach our table.

"Aye but not that guy," and we giggle together, "Fuck it, Jager time? Where's Emily? She never misses out."

"Outside on the phone. I'll order, you grab her?"

Stepping outside, I don't see her among the crowd in the smoking area, so I walk around the side of the club. Still no sign. I hear a noise in the alley, and as I edge toward it, my body stills, unable to move. The intensity of the anger I see before me scares me and I let out a gasp. The hooded figure stops and looks in my direction. I can't see his face, but I feel his glare all over me. I step back and try to turn to leave.

He is instantly on me, my back flush against his body. He has one hand wrapped around my waist, the other covering my mouth. Standing over a foot taller than me, he rests his chin on my head. My heart begins to race out of my chest, and I feel myself starting to hyperventilate as the panic kicks in.

He leans down and whispers ever so gently into my ear, "Breathe." I can't, my chest hurts from trying, so much so that I begin to feel a little light headed. "Deep breaths. It's ok, little one. I'm going to let you go and you're going back inside to your friends. You don't mention what happened here. Do you hear me? Nod if you understand."

I'm terrified but knowing I need to acknowledge what he has said, I nervously nod. "That's my good girl, I would never hurt you. Never. Now go". He doesn't need to tell me twice, and as soon as his grip loosens, I move as fast as my legs will carry me, never even looking back.

Breathless, I return inside just as Emily and Jenna land back at the table with the drinks. "So much for finding her, looks like you found someone though," Jenna laughs as she winks at me.

"Erm ... I... what?" I stutter.

"The ruffled hair and the flush on your face babe, you certainly look like you enjoyed yourself whoever he was."

I just shrug it off with a laugh neither confirming or denying what she is hinting at. We clink our glasses together as Emily films her customary boomerang video. I gulp the liquid down in one go, hoping it will help to settle the strange feeling running rampant in my body.

I'm not entirely sure why I didn't just tell them what happened. As terrified as I was, I think on some level I truly believed him, when he said he wouldn't hurt me. There was something all too familiar about him.

We finish our drinks and grab a takeaway on the way home. The taxi ride consists of chatter until the car stops outside my building. I hug the girls tight. "Remember, text when you get home." It's always been our tradition after a night out. No one settles until the last person is home.

"We know, safe and sound," Jenna shouts as I get out of the car.

"We love you bitch." Emily smiles and blows me a kiss.

Very dramatically I pretend to catch it in my right hand. "Love you too, girls" I shout back and turn towards the door.

I no more than get inside the front door and my phone beeps. With no chance they are home yet, I smile. As I open my phone the message is from an unknown number.

> UNKNOWN:
> Are you always so obedient?

> **Me:**
> Who is this?

> **UNKNOWN:**
> If anyone else was giving you orders tonight, I am not going to be happy.

Panic kicks in, as I stare at the words on my phone. Holy shite, it's the guy from outside the bar. How the fuck did he get my number? I may have felt an odd familiarity from him then, but this slightly scares me. Although, it also slightly intrigues me. Fueled by the alcohol in my system, I get a little brave.

> **Me:**
> Is that so? And just what would you do about it?

> **UNKNOWN:**
> *grinning squinting emoji* Well now, that's easy. I'd kill him. Nice to see you haven't lost your feistiness though. Good night Nora!

Oh boy, I'm in trouble.

Chapter Nine

Aodhán

Well, that was unexpected. When I sent the first message, I did not think for one second that she would engage with me. To be honest, I was only testing the water, but her response was nothing short of outstanding. Her fiery nature is the warm glow missing in my life. This was certainly not how I thought tonight was going to end when I left Oscar's earlier.

Arriving at Oscar's to pick up the cameras, he greeted me at the door. "Alright big lad, are you sure you don't want me to set these up for you?"

"Nah, mate, just show me how to install them. I need to keep them from being seen and then I want to be able to access the feed remotely from my phone."

He smiled and then replied, "No bother." After an hour and a couple of run throughs, with some very technical instructions, I was on my way to Nora's. It didn't take a lot of effort to get into her apartment building. A simple buzz to one of her neighbours *advising them I had a parcel for delivery, and I was inside no bother. Her lock was a little more difficult to navigate, taking me much longer than I expected, and yet, still too easy for her safety.*

Quietly closing her front door behind me, I turned towards the hall and her scent was everywhere. I closed my eyes and soak it in. Knowing my time was limited, I set about getting the cameras installed throughout the house. Setting one up on her bookcase, I took note of the titles, in particular those that looked read. I still needed to pick up a few, all in the name of research, of course.

Entering her bedroom, I took a moment to lie down on her bed and take a deep breath on her pillow. Her intoxicating smell is more intense here. I could just live here lost in her scent. Again. I reminded myself I needed to get moving, but not before I had a poke around her drawers. Lots of dainty lacy underwear, that I can't wait to peel off her beautiful body. All in good time.

Leaving her bedroom with one final glance, I spied a pair of black underwear on the top of her wash basket. Picking them up and lifting them to my face, the soft scent of apple blossoms and warm summer rain completely engulfed my mind. I decided to take them with me, and I slipped them into my jeans pocket as I headed towards the front door.

I hadn't been home to my own house since the night I was arrested, and wasn't quite ready to head back there. Next time I go home, Nora is coming with me, so I went to Mac's place instead.

The house was in darkness bar the soft glow coming from his office at the back of the house. He was crouched over, head in his hands and papers strewn across the desk. With a gentle rap on the door frame, I made my presence known.

His head shot up so fast, I was concerned he'd give himself whiplash. His facial expression softened as his eyes settled on me. "Nice to see you finally showing your face, where have you been?" *His words were laced with equal measures of suspicion and curiosity.*

"It's good to see you too, big brother, did you miss me?" *I flashed a big grinning smile right back at him.*

"You feckin' eejit, I'm glad you're home," *he remarked as he crossed the room pulling me in for a hug and a sharp thump on the back.*

"Yeah, me too, any chance of a beer?"

"Fine. But you may start talking. How are we getting Shadows' sorted? There is a lot of work needed and have you even thought about the opening?"

Shadows is our first venture into owning and running a club by ourselves. We'd taken over my father's territory including the running of the existing estate but this was going to be completely ours from the get go. Our centre of operations.

Whilst the work had begun to rejuvenate the old site, we hadn't really decided on how we were going to launch the club before I was lifted, but now I have an idea.

"Mac, we always get things done. I know this is the first one that's actually ours, but it will be grand, and yes, I have thought about the opening. What do you think about a VIP masquerade *ball? It fits the gothic nature of the venue and would be the talk of the city"*

I can see the cogs turning in that brain of his, his fingers running through his dark beard. His pondering means he thinks it's a good idea. Mac is well known for calling bullshit and calling it quickly. When he takes a beat before responding, you know he's trying to find a way to say it's good without offering the credit. Big softie.

"Aye, I suppose that could work. Right, leave it with me I'll sort the PR and Marketing you just get me a legit contractor to do the work, and Aodh, I mean legit no feckin' cowboys." I can sense the sigh in his last statement. It only happened once, some smickers owed me a favour after digging them out of a hole. They completely fucked up the job and despite it being years ago he's never let me forget it.

Before I could respond my phone pinged. The cameras in Nora's apartment activated the app on my phone. "Don't worry Mac, I'll get the best contractors available I promise. You just make sure we are good to go with everything else," I called back as I headed towards the spare room.

I flicked open the app and sure enough the live feed is running perfectly and I see Nora settling in on her sofa with a glass of wine. I laid back on the bed just watching the footage and marvelled at her beauty. The quality of the images are really great. I must remember to thank Oscar again.

SEEN

Suddenly Nora is up and getting dressed like she is heading out. Naughty little minx. So much for the quiet night in, I think as I leave the house and jump into my car.

I arrived at Nora's just as the taxi pulled up. Talk about good timing. I followed behind and watched as the car pulled in beside the Blackfort. I drove into the lay by across the street as she got out and greeted her friends. She looks stunning in a pair of jeans that perfectly hug that ass. I pulled my car into the car park behind and headed inside to try to get to a vantage point where I could see her but she wouldn't notice me.

She looked so good on the dance floor I almost made my way over to her but then some stupid bastard thought he'd have a go and put his hands on her. I could barely contain my rage as he leeched all over her, but then she shoved him out of the way and went to the bar just like my feisty good girl. I was going to leave it there and just continue to watch her, but he had to open his mouth calling her a cock tease as he passed by me. No one talks shit about what's mine.

I followed him outside and dragged him down the nearby alley. I laid into him, punch after punch, he had no idea why, and I didn't care, even when he fell to the ground. He lay in a bloody heap at my feet when I heard that gasp, I never expected to see her standing there. My hoodie obscured my face, so she had no idea it was me, and when I grabbed her, I almost dragged her to my car and home.

Bastard got what he deserved. He dared to run his scummy hands all over what belongs to me. She is mine and no one touches her but me.

I'm still amazed she didn't mention what happened, never mind the brave and cheeky message she replied with. Interestingly, she didn't respond to the last message though. Switching over to the camera app, I see her.

She is lying back on her bed with her legs dangling over the side, phone in her hands, held just above her face like she is just staring at it. Is she considering a response? I turn up the volume, but the only audio I'm greeted by is just silence.

Setting the phone down by her side she sits up and begins to remove her boots. Something so simple and the sight of it triggers a shot right to my cock. I release it from my boxers and grab her panties from my jeans.

As I watch her discard the boots and begin to open the buttons on her jeans, I lift her panties to my face and inhale her delicious scent. I long for the day when I can touch her, taste her, and the thought of her, has me twirling the panties around my fingers and reaching for my cock–rock hard and begging for her touch.

I begin to stroke myself. The coarse feel of the lace along my skin is exhilarating and amazing. She peels the jeans down her legs so slowly it's almost erotic, she kicks them off and I continue to stroke myself, gripping ever so slightly harder, the sight of her turning me on so much more.

She reaches for the hem of her top and drags it slowly over her head before falling back to the bed. I imagine myself leaning over her and kissing her body from toe to her knee, to her inner thigh, and up to her soft centre. Stroking faster as my imagination takes hold, precum begins to pool on the tip. I swipe my thumb across it and down my shaft coating myself and tugging faster.

Closing my eyes I see her mouth, those full soft lips parted slightly as she kisses the tip of my cock before sucking me in and engulfing my entire length. I'm so lost in the vision I begin stroking faster and I feel the familiar tightening of my balls, my release so close, losing control, I grip tighter and move my hand, still wrapped in her panties, up and down even faster. With her name, simply a whisper on my lips, I come undone and pour my release into her pretty black lace panties.

Opening my eyes, I smile. This won't be the last pair of her panties that I ruin with my cum.

Chapter Ten

Nora

Vaguely aware of the noises from outside, I draw my hands to my head and push my fingers firmly against my temples. Why did I drink so much last night? This hangover is awful. Slowly, I swing my legs around and over the edge of the bed, bringing myself to a sitting position, and allow my eyes to adjust to the daylight streaming in through the gap in my blinds. I dread to think how early it must be.

Dragging myself down the hall and into the kitchen, I notice a familiar scent I can't place. Looking around the room I'm unable to put my finger on what it could be. It's faint but distinctive all the same. Reaching the sink, I pour myself a pint of water and neck it in one go. The cooling sensation runs down my throat and I can feel it as it hits my stomach. Right on cue, it begins to rumble.

History tells me that although my stomach is crying out for sustenance right now, it won't handle more than some toast. So toast it is. Waiting for it to pop, I drudge back down the hall to my bedroom to grab my phone. I remember most of the night but getting home is a little hazy and the hangover fear kicks in. *Please don't say I did anything stupid.*

Unlocking the phone, I notice it opens directly into a chat with an unknown number and the memory hits me with force. The hooded guy outside the bar and the sinister messages. Hangover fear transforms into total panic. That smell, I think I recognize it, but how can it be here? I cautiously move from room to room checking carefully but there is no one else in the apartment and yet that smell lingers in each room. Maybe I am going mad.

Shaking off the uneasy feeling, I message the girls to see how things are this morning.

> **Me:**
> Does anyone else feel like they drank the Sahara desert last night?

> **Emily:**
> Nope! I'm fresh as a daisy this morning *star-struck emoji* Heading for a hike up Divis Mountain if either of you fancy it?

Jenna:

Are you serious right now? No thanks. I'm hurting badly. I'm just going to chill in my jammies for the day. Nora, don't you have that date tonight though?

Me:

OMG! *screaming in fear emoji* I completely forgot about that. I am soo not going to that. I just need to find a way to blow him off.

Emily:

Yeah I bet you'd like to blow him off all right *winking emoji* You've been single for sooooo long, come on it's only one drink. What could possibly go wrong?

Me:

Eugh no! I really don't want to. I don't know that I could even face a drink right now.

SEEN

> **Jenna:**
> Nonsense. Shower, food and you'll be grand. Seriously though, what have you got to lose? It could be fun.

> **Me:**
> Maybe. I'll keep you posted.

I know they mean well but I'm not sure I want to do this. The jury is still out on whether I'm going, but perhaps Jenna is right. Food and a shower might be the cure.

Despite my better judgement, later that evening, I find myself sitting in the bar waiting for Ollie to arrive. Time passes watching the people around me and reading through the chat from 'Unknown', but then my mind wanders back to the fella from the coffee shop. He was something else.

I look up from my phone as Ollie arrives. Sweet but awkward greetings as he motions to kiss my cheek before ordering us a round of drinks. Oddly, the conversation comes easy as he talks about his job and his hobbies. Interestingly, he plays football for a local club. *I do love a man in short shorts.*

We talk for hours, and as natural as it feels, there is no real spark there. I know they say the spark isn't everything, and maybe I've read too many romance novels, but I'm just not feeling this. I could just as easily be sitting talking to a friend. When he heads to the restroom, I take the opportunity to check my phone. Maybe I can get the girls to call and give me my out without having to let him down face to face. Before I can even get that far I see a message from 'Unknown'.

> **UNKNOWN:**
> Naughty girl, Nora. Do you realise what you have done?

I should be terrified but something about the anonymous nature of the sender, not to mention the 'Naughty girl' comment has butterflies swarming my stomach. This guy beat the shit of some random guy outside a bar last night.

Come to think of it, that was the guy leering all over me on the dance floor.

Shit. Is he here?

My eyes dart around the room trying to find someone watching me. I don't even know what, or who, I'm looking for. I never saw his face and I doubt I'd know him even if I did see him.

When Ollie returns, I make my apologies and leave as fast as I can, trying to grab the first cab I can find outside. I just want to be in the safety of my own home. My heart is racing when my phone pings again and I know before I even look that it's *him*.

> **UNKNOWN:**
> You can run, but you can't hide!

SEEN

> **Me:**
> Who are you and what do you want with me?

> **UNKNOWN:**
> You'll find out soon enough, little one!

Standing at the edge of the pavement, watching up and down the road, waiting to flag down a cab, I feel two large hands grab my shoulders and drag me backwards into the darkness between the two buildings. A hand covers my mouth stopping me from screaming. My eyes are desperately trying to adjust to the darkness, trying to focus on the person in front of me. My mind automatically assumes this is 'Unknown'. When he said soon, I didn't think he meant this soon.

"Little one, did you really think you could go on a date, and I wouldn't find out?" His voice is muffled slightly but his words are crystal clear. He was watching me. His face still obscured from my vision, I try to respond but his hand holds my face so tightly that I can't move my mouth.

He leans in and whispers into my ear. "You are mine, my réaltín álainn." My eyes widen in shock, I know those words. Where the fuck do I know those words from? I stop struggling as I'm frantically searching through the crevices of my mind while my eyes do the same with his face. I still can't make it out, but the memory clicks. *Coffee shop guy.*

He clocks the shift in my demeanour and laughs, "So you do recognise those words, don't you? Do you know how I have longed to touch you?"

He removes his hand from my mouth just enough that I can speak. "What the actual fuck? Couldn't you just ask me out like a normal person?"

He smiles, "I tried once but you rudely declined. Anyways, where is the fun in that? Besides, given your reading history, I thought you liked the darkness."

My reading history? How long has he been watching me? That's when it hits me–his smell, the same one I sensed this morning in my apartment. He was in my apartment; of that, I am absolutely sure now. Frustration takes over and I retort, "I may read dark romance, and enjoy the downright dirty and depraved things that are written, but that is not real and it certainly doesn't mean I want that in real life. Fiction is an escape from reality."

Caged between his arms, he leans in again and I take a deep breath trying to settle myself. He is so intoxicating, I almost passed out. He moves his right arm and traces the lines of my face. I wish I could touch him. Despite myself, I really want to feel him.

His face is just millimetres from my face and with that deep chocolatey smooth voice whispers, "Your heartbeat and breathing give you away, little one. Don't worry, I'll show you just how dark and depraved you really like it." He glides his tongue along my throat. "I wonder if the rest of you tastes as delicious".

He steps back and turns in the opposite direction. "I'll see you real soon," he laughs and with that, he's gone.

I'm a walking fucking contradiction–slightly terrified, very intrigued, and utterly soaked. What the fuck is wrong with me? Gathering my composure, I pull myself together and flag down a taxi to take me home.

Sitting safely in the back of the cab, I replay the whole interaction and wonder just how soon it will be before I see him again.

Waking up the next morning when my alarm goes off, I struggle to open my eyes. My eyelids are heavy and my head hurts, not so much from the drinking, but the vivid dreams of the night before. The dreams of *him*.

I climb out of bed and drag myself to the shower trying to shake off the flashes of dream fragments. The cold water shocks my system and I become fully aware. *Wise up, Nora.* I urge myself to forget it and concentrate on the day ahead. I'm booked in for a nice relaxing massage, and I can't wait.

I arrive early for my appointment and the receptionist shows me to the treatment room. Handling me a towel and a robe. "I'll be back in 5 minutes to allow you to get ready," she says with a smile.

"Thanks."

I close the door behind her and look around the room. There are candles lining the shelves and incense burning. The smells are delicious–lavender and chamomile–while the gentle wind chimes music plays ever so softly.

I undress and climb on the table with the towel draped over my legs and back. Lowering my head into the hole at the top of the bed, I close my eyes waiting for the young girl to return.

I hear the sound of the door opening and then closing. The footsteps sound heavier than I would have expected, but I don't pay much heed to that as the towel is pulled gently off my back.

I feel the warm oil being poured along my spine and it feels glorious. Fingertips trace along my spine through the oil starting to spread it across my back. It's then that the fingertips become hands, large rough hands roaming all over my back and edging along my sides.

These do not feel like the hands of the young girl who brought me in. I shuffle on the bed, attempting to lift my arms to help me raise my head. The person moves and I catch a glimpse of big work boots just as I feel warm air by my ear.

"Don't scream, little one. If you wanted a massage all you had to do was ask, because I will not tolerate anyone else touching your body. You are mine."

My brain is screaming at me to open my mouth, to move to do something, but my body is frozen as he continues to run his hands up and down my back, his fingers slipping down my sides and along the edges of my breasts.

SEEN

I know this is wrong, but fuck, it feels so right. I can't help but love the feel of his hands on my skin. It makes me tingle, and the way he said I was his, in that deep possessive manner, lit my core on fire.

His hands move down my body as he removes the towel completely. I am face down naked in front of the man I was dreaming about last night and yet I still can't bring myself to move. His fingers run up my legs and dig into my thighs as his breathing becomes more ragged.

He nudges the insides of my legs and commands me to open them, the gravelled raspiness of his voice has me obeying without even thinking. "Good girl." His praise elicits a moan from me that I can't contain.

Pouring more oil on my skin he massages the top of my thighs and skims the curves of my ass, creeping closer and closer to between my legs. It feels so good that when he shifts, sliding his hand under me, and strokes my pussy, I find myself lifting my hips to allow him better access.

I want him to touch me, and as if he hears my silent plea, he runs his fingers along my slit and circles my clit. Panting at the feel of his hands on me, and the ragged breathing from behind me, I begin to grind on his hand. He shoves two fingers inside me and his other hand traces along my back and up my neck to grip my hair.

He holds my head in place, the pressure of his fingers wrapped around my hair tightening as he fucks my pussy with his other hand, has me so turned on that I am a panting mess.

He picks up the pace and I groan as I feel my orgasm building. He rubs my clit and I crash over the edge I've been teetering on.

His grip on my hair eases and he removes his hand from under me. I feel his teeth trail across my left bum cheek before he plants a kiss on it. "This was fun, little one. I can't wait until next time. See you soon."

I lie there on the table, spent, relaxed and confused all at once. My brain is desperately trying to piece together what just happened. When I finally convince my body to move, I get dressed quicker than I ever have done before. Stepping out of the treatment room, I can feel the embarrassment rising on my face. The young girl from earlier, smiles like she knows exactly what just happened in that room.

I run out of the shop as fast as my feet can take me. Exhilarated and mortified.

Chapter Eleven

Aodhán

I had to tear myself away. It's not time yet, but I couldn't resist getting that close and touching her. The thought of someone else running their fingers over that body, even if it was some wee girl just doing her job just riled me.

I didn't mean for it to go even that far, but the feel of her skin and that moan she let out when I traced the curve of her cheeks, made me want so much more. The feel of her clenching my fingers when she came made my cock so fucking hard, I almost came there and then.

I sucked my fingers dry devouring every drop of her sweet juices. It's a taste I will never be able to get enough of. I am completely hooked on this woman, and I can only hope and pray that she is willing to accept me, because I am not giving her up. She is my addiction and I don't want to ever recover from her.

It took monumental self control to walk out of that room and leave her lying there, but it won't be long until I have my hands on her again, and possess every inch of her body and consume her.

The next few days pass without incident. Nora has sequestered herself in her apartment, and I'm starting to think perhaps I've taken this whole thing too far. Maybe I should have just approached her normally, but it was so much fun watching her from the darkness. It's usually my comfort zone. With her out of reach for now, I've had to settle for watching the camera footage in between meetings with Mac and Riley around the opening of Shadows.

We have run security and protection for clubs all over Belfast for years now, but we wanted a place of our own. The contractors have been working all weekend doing the renovations and we are on track for opening night. It's a bigger night for me than the boys. This will be the night I make my move. The night I've been waiting for, since stepping out of the prison van and laying my eyes on her for the very first time.

Riley chose the décor and somehow, he managed to capture the essence correctly. Dark and gothic architecture, with obscure little alcoves built towards the back. A huge bar is located in the centre of the downstairs with seating areas to one side and an open dance floor to the other, steps leading down onto it. Stairs at the front door lead to the balconies overlooking the dance floor and more seating.

Towards the back of the club, there is a secret staircase behind a bookcase that leads to the private rooms downstairs only accessible by us. It's where we will run the entire operation from now. We each have our own office, and there is the security room covered with monitors that will display the security camera footage which covers every inch of the building.

The kitchen is state of the art and the bar will be fully stocked. The intention is to run as a restaurant throughout the week, and as a club on the weekends.

We chose this place as it overlooks the Lagan River and at nighttime, you can see the twinkling lights across Belfast. The Arena, Titanic building, and the historic Samson and Goliath are all within view towering over the skyline. We added two outdoor areas, one on the lower level with tables and chairs, perfect for summer afternoons. Well, they would be if we ever got summer weather in this bloody country.

The second area was all my idea, it's a sweeping decked balcony area accessible from the upper levels inside and will be perfect at nighttime. It wasn't easy getting that idea passed the boys, not with the eejits around Belfast and the fact that if you wanted to, you could use it as a diving board straight into the river. It will be interesting to see what Health and Safety make of it during the inspection tomorrow. But if we pull it off, it will be the selling point for function bookings.

Opening night will be a masquerade ball, and I have the perfect idea to get Nora here. It will truly be a night to remember if the contractor can get the paintwork finished on time. Mac has done a great job on the marketing and the guest list is full including the three little names I snuck in.

Well, my girl won't come on her own, and her friends are unlikely to want to miss out on a night at the hottest new club in town. Or, so I hope. Just have to add a few finishing touches to my plan.

"Mac, I gotta run, you ok here?"

He glares at me. "Where are you going? There is a shite load of work to do here."

I grin. "Going to the Moy for a load of canaries."

His face is a picture, the rage bubbling up in him to bursting point. "Canaries? Are you serious right now? We are two days away from opening and you want to get canaries? I'm not having birds flying about this place."

I can hardly breathe for laughing. "Chill Bro, it's just a saying, like, 'I'm away to see a man about a dog' or whatever. Basically, I'm going out and not telling you where I'm going."

"What sort of fucking saying are either of those things, canaries and dogs? Can't you ever just speak straight for fuck's sake?" His face is pure red with anger. I really should have known better to poke the bear, but it delights me so much to do so. I head for the door, and I catch Riley hiding in one of the alcoves crouched over holding his stomach, a moment of panic passes through me until I realise he is laughing too. I pat him on the back. "Breathe, wee man."

"Stop, seriously! I literally can't fucking catch a breath" He barely gets out before starting to laugh all over again. Who'd have thought such a simple saying would send my brothers to the opposite ends of the spectrum; one so incensed, and the other with a serious dose of giggles? I leave laughing to myself, and they call me the crazy one of us.

Leaving Shadows, I realise I still have so much to organise for my own opening night. I can't wait to finally get her in my arms, even if I have to steal her away. She has become my obsession, my light in the darkness. The last few days have been agony, but thankfully there isn't long to wait as the first part of my plan is almost in place.

I can only hope she is open to the idea.

Chapter Twelve

Nora

Following the crazy weekend, I have enjoyed the quiet serenity of being at home. He has invaded my every thought over the last few days. I've lifted my phone to message him so many times. I can't even put my finger on what has stopped me. I should have been terrified by his obsessive behaviour and the fact that he seems to know exactly where I am at all times. He's been in my apartment, and not to mention what happened at the massage place but somewhere deep down I recognise I'm not afraid. What's worse is I'm intrigued and scarily excited to see what's next.

There is something safe about him. Obsessive and possessive perhaps, but he has made no attempt to harm me. *What is wrong with me?* I begin to question why I can't just meet men in a normal fashion, and then I remember the day outside the coffee shop. He stood so tall, towering over me with those broad shoulders and that delicious smell as he asked me to go for a coffee. A chance interaction, or was it? Perhaps one day, I'll find out.

Trying to distract myself from thinking about him, I drag myself back into the book I'm reading. Yes, it's a stalker romance novel. Maybe I manifested him after reading so many of these books. Damn it, there I go again thinking about him.

A knock at the door startles me, I put down my book and make my way to the door. As I open the front door there is no one there, I lean out and look up and down the hall, but I can't see anyone. I do, however, see a very large black gift box with a silver bow. I have no idea what it could be, and I scour my memory trying to find some insight as to whether I maybe ordered something while drunk, but I come up short.

Curiously, I lift the box which seems to have a bit of weight within and bring it inside. Setting it on the dining room table, I stare at it for a few minutes before nervously opening it. Nestled on top of the black tissue paper is a large silver envelope, with my name beautifully written on the outside.

Inside the envelope is a VIP invitation to a masquerade ball, being held on the opening night of the new club in town. I flip it over and there is nothing else. No indication of where it came from. I read that opening night was due to be all celebrities and influencers, so how in the hell am I on the list? And not only that, but I have two plus ones.

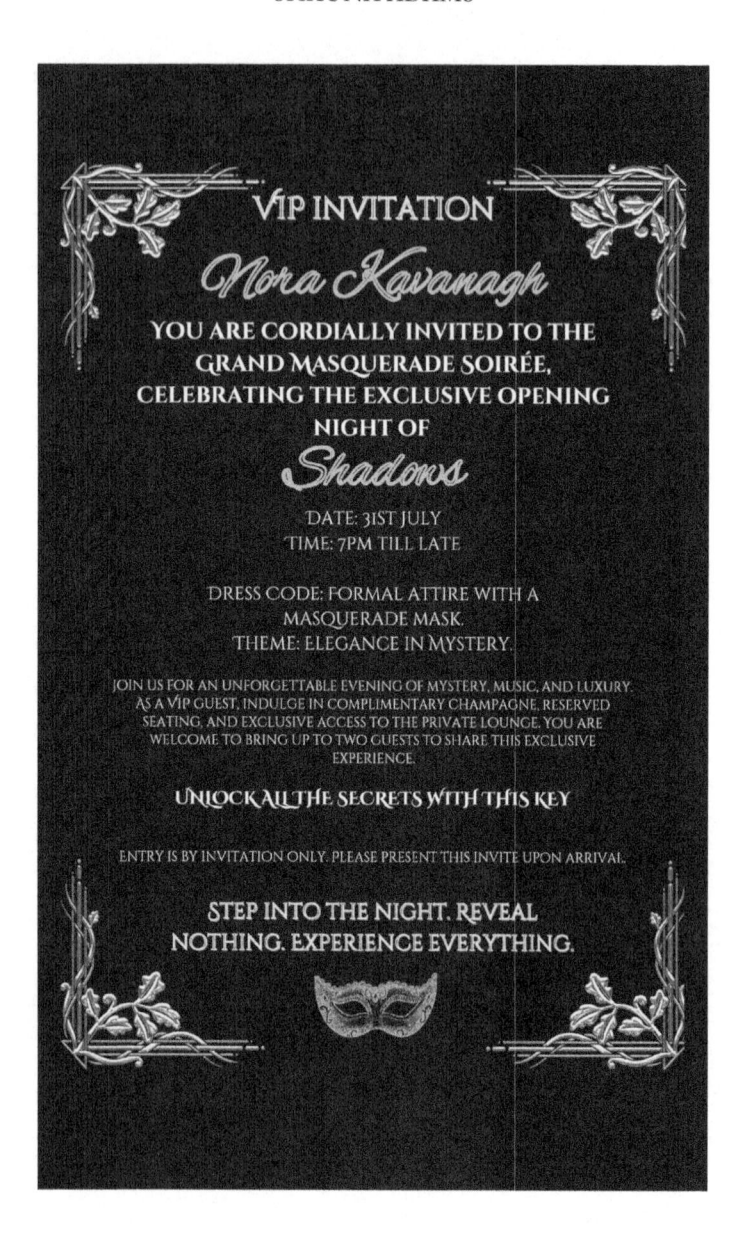

VIP INVITATION

Nora Kavanagh

YOU ARE CORDIALLY INVITED TO THE GRAND MASQUERADE SOIRÉE, CELEBRATING THE EXCLUSIVE OPENING NIGHT OF

Shadows

DATE: 31ST JULY
TIME: 7PM TILL LATE

DRESS CODE: FORMAL ATTIRE WITH A MASQUERADE MASK.
THEME: ELEGANCE IN MYSTERY.

JOIN US FOR AN UNFORGETTABLE EVENING OF MYSTERY, MUSIC, AND LUXURY. AS A VIP GUEST, INDULGE IN COMPLIMENTARY CHAMPAGNE, RESERVED SEATING, AND EXCLUSIVE ACCESS TO THE PRIVATE LOUNGE. YOU ARE WELCOME TO BRING UP TO TWO GUESTS TO SHARE THIS EXCLUSIVE EXPERIENCE.

UNLOCK ALL THE SECRETS WITH THIS KEY

ENTRY IS BY INVITATION ONLY. PLEASE PRESENT THIS INVITE UPON ARRIVAL.

STEP INTO THE NIGHT. REVEAL NOTHING. EXPERIENCE EVERYTHING.

SEEN

I almost forgot that the envelope isn't the only thing in the box. I carefully pull back the tissue paper to find the most exquisite emerald, green lace ball gown. I hold it up and admire the beautifully intricate lace bodice and free-flowing skirt. It is by far the most elegant dress I have ever seen. Something I would have dreamed of, but never bought for myself.

Looking back into the box I also find an emerald and silver mask with sequins in the shape of starbursts. Nothing else to indicate who the sender is. I do wonder though, could it be him?

Still trying to work out what is going on, I pull out my phone and take a picture of the dress, mask, and the invite and send it to the girls. They are going to freak out when they see this. We've been talking about this new club for ages and there aren't two other people I'd rather take with me.

Within seconds my phone is ringing with a group video call, right on cue. The first voice I hear is Emily squealing with delight, "What the actual fuck? That is stunning! Oh girl, you are going to be one hot mama in that dress"

"Bitch that invite says 2 guests, you better be taking us?" Jenna never misses a detail.

Trying desperately not to get too carried away, "Girls, calm down. I don't even know if I'm going to go. This is so weird. I've no idea who this is from."

"I will drag you kicking and screaming. VIP night, free champagne, let's do this. Tell her, Jenna."

"Too right, this is going to be the hottest club in town. Imagine the experience and who cares who sent it! We'll be with you, so it's going to be epic. You're not turning this down." Jenna stares down the camera lens and it feels like she is staring right into my soul.

I think for a moment, maybe the girls are right. I mean, it couldn't hurt, right? Maybe I'll find out who my mystery sender is. Who knows, maybe it's the coffee shop guy, and maybe he actually listened?

I look back to the camera, roll my eyes and declare, "Fuck it, let's do it. This is going to be an epic night, so let's go and enjoy it." I laugh as they whoop and cheer. We then spent the next half hour discussing hair, makeup, what they were going to wear, and debating on whether this was all down to the coffee shop guy.

Initially, the girls were pretty freaked out at the idea that my super-hot coffee shop guy had turned into my 'stalker'. After the interaction following my date with Ollie, I broke and called an emergency girl talk meeting to spill the craic.

As expected, Emily was out for blood. She is fiercely protective of those closest to her and she will literally go to war for any one of us. Jenna was slightly reserved at the beginning, but that's not beyond the norm for her. She has always been the type of person to sit back and take in everything before adding her two cents to the conversation.

Maybe it was the way I told the story, maybe it was the many cocktails consumed or perhaps it was simply the way I was 'grinning like the cat that got the cream' by the end, but the girls were slightly more relaxed by the time we were saying our goodbyes.

Waving them off that night, I slumped into bed having just about gotten my jammies on and drifted off to sleep, dreaming of my mystery man.

Having determined our preparations for the ball, we said our goodbyes and ended the video call. I lie back on the chair in my living room, my head dropping over the edge as I draw in a long breath trying to calm myself. Excitement and a hint of trepidation runs through my body. Sitting forward after a few minutes, I pull my hands up to my face and drag them back down before looking over to the beautiful gown now hanging on the back of my door.

Am I really going to do this? Closing my eyes, I take another deep breath and then my phone pings.

> Coffee Shop Guy:
> I hope you liked my little gift!

> Me:
> Dude, Seriously? Why?

> **Coffee Shop Guy:**
>
> Why what? Why did I send you a gift? I think that is pretty self explanatory, don't you?

> **Me:**
>
> No, I don't. Why did you send this to me? What is going on?

> **Coffee Shop Guy:**
>
> Is it really such a mystery to you? Come to the party and, just maybe, you will get the answers you seek.

> **Me:**
>
> Do I at least get to know your name now? I feel like I'm at such a disadvantage here and I don't like it one bit.

> **Coffee Shop Guy:**
>
> Show up and I promise I will answer all your questions.

Oh boy he is not going to make this easy on me, is he? I guess, there is no going back now.

Chapter Thirteen

Nora

Work dragged something rotten the last two days. I haven't heard anything further from Coffee Shop Guy since our message exchange after the gift box arrived. My anxiety has been continually increasing and is close to reaching epic levels to the point where I am seriously considering not going.

This guy could be a murderer for all I know. I may have felt a sense of safety during our recent interactions, but what if that was just the alcohol talking. I've never been one to act so impulsively. I enjoy nights out with my girls, but I've never had a serious relationship, or a relationship of any kind. Oh god, what am I talking about, I don't even know if that's what he wants.

Maybe I am just overthinking this whole thing, it's not like I haven't indulged in one night stands before. I'm not a prude. I guess, I just always wanted someone to still want me the next morning. It just never worked out that way.

Just then, I hear the familiar sound of knocking on my door. As I open the door I'm greeted with my two best friends squealing with excitement and somehow it eases my anxiety a little.

Jenna pours us glasses of bubbly while Emily gets to work transforming me. Thanks to straighteners and curling tongs, half an hour later my hair is looking stunning, even if I do say so myself. It's styled in a split updo, half pinned up in a messy bun while the rest falls slightly over my shoulder in soft curls. My makeup is on point, beautifully flawless green and black eyeshadow, and magic mascara has lengthened my eyelashes to the point where it actually looks like I already have fake ones on. I must remember to get the name of that one from her.

Spinning around in the chair, I see Jenna's grinning face and I know I must look good. I'm the type of person who doesn't get dolled up for no reason, so when I do, I always look like a completely different person. I just don't see the point of this type of effort on a daily basis.

Hair and makeup done, I slip into my elegant ball gown and am pleasantly surprised at how it just hugs my curves perfectly. It's like this dress was made just for me. Which in itself is a miracle, I always have problems trying to get dresses to fit so perfectly, and it makes me curious as to how he did this.

Waiting for the girls to get into their dresses, I pour us some shots. Dutch courage and all that. I need something a little stronger than prosecco to settle the nerves. I knock one back and by the time I have another poured, the girls are dressed and have joined me. We hit the shots and take a few selfies as well as Emily's beloved boomerangs, before heading out of the apartment and into our taxi.

Chapter Fourteen

Aodhán

Watching the camera, I see her agonise over what to do and then like the good little girl she is, she starts to get ready. I'm glad the girls are there with her, they will keep her level enough to ensure she gets here. Watching her this past week, I could see her nerves were threatening to get the better of her.

I know the feeling. I am finding it very difficult to settle. I tried not to watch the footage once she moved to put the dress on. I want to see her in all her glory up close and in person. I'm pacing back and forth in the office watching the cameras over the front door. The girls left Nora's house over an hour ago and they still haven't arrived. I knew I should have sent a car.

Mac is out in the bar area greeting some of the VIPs, but there is only one I care about. The music is pumping and the clientele is top tier. The boys did a great job on the promotion. Shadows is certainly going to be the hottest place in town after tonight.

SEEN

The office door opens and diverts my attention away from the cameras. "Would you ever fucking settle yourself? Everything is sorted, guests are arriving and it's going to be great," Mac laughs. I'm amazed he is so chill tonight, considering his outburst earlier in the week.

"I have a VIP of my own due tonight and she is not fucking here yet!" I blurt without thinking. As soon as the words tumble out of my mouth, I stop dead where I stand. *Fuck*.

"Ah, right. Now that explains a lot." He smacks me on the back. "So little brother, who is the mysterious woman who has the great Aodhán O'Neill's kecks in a twist?" His laugh now bellowing around the room.

"Fuck off Mac, just concentrate on your own little project and leave me to mine."

Just then, my phone buzzes. She's here. Her ticket was flagged to alert me the moment it was scanned.

Time to find my réaltín álainn.

Chapter Fifteen

Nora

Arriving at the club, we step out of the taxi and straight onto the red carpet. I feel like such an imposter. *How did I end up here?* I feel nauseous. Jenna senses my hesitancy and grabs my hand. I instantly feel better. Emily reminds me we were invited, and we should enjoy it. With their reassurances, I shake off the nerves and feel myself becoming more confident as we strut our stuff all the way to the front door.

Gazing around the club as we pass through the front door, I notice the dark, gothic aesthetic–it is gorgeous. Moving further into the club we see the dance floor, strobe lighting, and smoke machine making it the focal point in the room downstairs.

The bar is lined with trays of champagne flutes and nibbles. We make a beeline for the drink and food. Drink now in hand, we find ourselves star-struck at all the local celebrities. The DJ stops the music and greets everyone; "Welcome one and all to

Shadows, let's party." The girls and I low-key squeal, making our way to the dance floor to boogie.

We spent the next couple of hours enjoying the celeb-watching, dancing, and soaking in the atmosphere. In the back of my mind, every time my eyes pan across the room and up to the balconies, I'm hoping to spot my Coffee Shop Guy. I start to wonder if the masks are obscuring his face or worst-case scenario, he didn't show at all. I resolve to enjoy the night with my girls, and hey, if he shows, he shows. If he doesn't, then at least I'll have had a night to remember anyway.

Downing another glass of the free champagne, Emily drags us back to the dance floor and we drop our moves. I don't initially notice as two hands are placed on my hips, but when I do I lean into them. Grinding on the mystery man behind, my confidence is buoyed by the booze and the attention. I attempt to turn around to see him, but he holds me in place firmly as his hands roam up and down my body.

I lean my head back into his chest and it's then I get that familiar smell, woody, spicy, and with a hint of citrus. I can barely contain my excitement as I recognize my coffee shop guy, the man who made me a panting mess on a massage table. He leans his head down into the groove in my neck and whispers into my ear–which was so fucking hot. "Hey beautiful, I'm delighted you decided to show up, now do you want to get out of here? I'm not sure I can keep my resolve much longer."

My eyes dart to the girls who are grinning back and forth between themselves and me. Jenna mouths to me, 'Is that him?'

I bite my lip before replying, 'Yes'. The two girls squeal between them and begin waving in my direction.

It gives me the confidence to nod my head and throw a quick wave at the girls as he pushes us towards the front door. "Text us later, bitch!" I hear them call in the distance over the music.

By the time we get outside, I finally see him, my Coffee Shop Guy. Dressed in a tight black tux, with a crisp white shirt that looks like it was painted on. His tie is the exact same colour as my dress. *Oh my god, he matched my dress*. I can see the muscles in his chest fighting to be released. This man must have been carved from marble by the gods and I grinded against him like I was a dog in heat. My anxiety kicks in and I'm about to change my mind.

"Don't do that," he declares quietly. "I can see your hesitancy, trust me. I promise you'll be safe. Come with me. I've been itching to get my hands on you, to taste that deliciously sweet pussy again"

Between the buzz of the alcohol, his intoxicating scent that invades my very being, that chiseled body, and the moistness building in my knickers, I smile. "Fuck it, let's go."

He takes me by the hand and walks me over to his black range rover with darkened windows. Opening the passenger door, he helps me up into the vehicle, taking care to lift the skirt of my dress, before getting into the driver seat beside me. He starts the engine and rests his hands on the steering wheel before looking towards me.

SEEN

I haven't taken my eyes off him this whole time. He reaches across, slips my mask off my head and runs his fingers down the side of my face, tracing his thumb across my lips. I feel like I could catch fire, the electricity between us is overwhelming. He turns back to the steering wheel, and we tear out of the car park and down the dark roads going who knows where.

I watch him as he drives, hands gripping the wheel like he is holding on for dear life. I lose all sense of direction and time, until we pull into a country lane. In the darkness it seems almost too small for us to even be on. He holds it steady until we reach where the road widens up slightly. Just ahead is the most beautiful house surrounded by tall evergreen trees.

I'm still looking around at the gardens and the house, as we stop. He jumps out and comes around to open my door. He reaches up with one hand to take mine and the other slides into the small of my back, it fits so effortlessly like it was made to be there. He guides me up the steps and into the house. He still hasn't spoken a word and I'm almost afraid to speak, as if it will break the enchantment surrounding us.

No sooner than we step inside, and the door closes behind us, he has me caged between his arms on the door with a look like he is about to completely devour me. "I have waited so long to have you here," he almost growls at me like it took every inch of strength to even say the words and I'm blushing. Through the heat of his body against mine, I can feel the desire dripping from him.

His rough calloused hand traces down the side of my face and settles on my throat. He holds me securely but not hard enough to choke me, staring into my eyes he leans in close enough to brush his lips across mine, a flick of his tongue along my top lip, and before I can breathe, his lips are crushing into mine in a kiss so intoxicating, I'm not sure I'll ever breathe freely again.

I'm completely lost in him.

Chapter Sixteen

Aodhán

It took every ounce of willpower not to drag her out of the club the moment she arrived. I waited and watched her enjoy the festivities with her friends, but then I couldn't wait any longer. I wasn't sure she was going to come with me.

Now, I have her whimpering in my mouth, with my hand wrapped around her throat. I'm completely and utterly fucked. There is no way I'm ever going to be able to let her go now.

She moans as I deepen our kiss telling me she is clearly as affected by me as I am by her. I break contact but only to say, "Get on your knees. I want to see if those lips are as good around my cock as they are on my mouth."

The look on her face suggests she wants to bite back, but she slides down the door and onto her knees. Reaching for my belt excruciatingly slowly, she drags it through each loop until it is no longer in my trousers, and she tosses it behind her.

She reaches back to my waist and starts to open my trousers, first the button and then glides the zip down with her teeth. *Fuck that is hot.* She slides her hand through the top of my boxers, slipping them down, and my cock springs out. She continues to pull them down to my ankles, never taking her eyes off me.

Staring deep into my eyes she sticks out her tongue and licks me from base to tip before drawing the head into her mouth. She runs her tongue around it, and–*fuck me*–I could just blow my load from this alone.

She eases back and my cock bounces from her mouth. She gives it a slight tug before moving to take the whole thing, right into the back of her throat and then she starts to move up and down swiping her tongue along the shaft.

I drop my head back just for a second, lost in the pleasure before looking back down at her. Fuck, she is beautiful, those blue eyes boring into mine as she sucks my cock is a sight I'll never tire of. I reach my hand around the back of her neck and into her hair before forcing my cock deeper into her throat, she gags slightly and tears run down the side of her face.

"Good girl, just like that." She moans in reply. Yes, my girl likes to be praised, and I am going to love worshipping her.

As her hand moves to cup my balls, I almost lose it right there. I pull back and out of her mouth lifting her to her feet, pinning her back on the door, and crushing into her mouth, hands running up and down her body.

I grab her ass and whisper in her ear, "It's time I got to taste that pretty little cunt of yours properly." I spin her around, so her chest is flush against the door, and I begin to undress her. I pull the zip down and let the dress fall to the ground before turning her back to face me.

I press my lips onto her and kiss her deeply before dropping to my knees and lifting her right leg over my shoulder. She is soaking wet, and man, she smells so delicious. And I'm fucking starved.

Chapter Seventeen

Nora

Holy sweet mother of fuck is all I can think as I feel his tongue run along my inner thigh before licking along my lower lips. He alternates between licks and sucks on my clit, eating me like a man possessed, like I'm his last meal and he can't get enough of me. As he slides two fingers into my pussy and strums me like an instrument, I can feel my orgasm starting to build.

"Oh my god!"

"Don't you dare even think of praising him for my hard work."

As I start to giggle, he adds another finger inside and it tips me over the edge. My orgasm hits me like a freight train and leaves me gasping for air. Who the fuck is this guy?

He sets my leg down and stands to devour my lips before pushing his fingers into my mouth. "See how good you taste, réaltín álainn. I've had that taste on my mind all week." I still have no idea what those words mean but the way he says them makes me so wet.

He kicks off his shoes and wriggles out of his trousers before lifting me bridal style. "I think we should try to make it to the bedroom this time," he says with a grin, and I realise he still has his mask on. He carries me with such ease, then again, he is built like a shit house. I smile to myself and reach up to remove his mask. He looks down at me and I admire the beautiful features on his face.

When we reach the bedroom, he gently drops me on the bed and kisses me again, he grabs my right nipple and tugs on it, twisting, as I gasp. He moves his mouth to the other nipple and runs his tongue around it, sucks, and then bites down hard. The pain is instant but fuck the pleasure is so much more when he drives two fingers deep into my pussy.

It's all I can do not to scream. One hand gripping my throat, fingers buried in my pussy, and his mouth devouring my nipple. I'm a soaking mess and then he withdraws leaving me panting and silently begging for more.

He steps back to grab a condom and once he is fully sheathed, he pulls me towards the end of the bed and lines his cock up with my entrance. With one thrust he buries himself in me and I scream out. He feels so good as he thrusts in and out while tugging on my nipples and crushing my lips in a bruising kiss.

Every nerve ending is on fire, and when he reaches down to pinch my clit I'm gone, sparks flying and my whole body is shaking. He stills momentarily while my orgasm flows over me and once it has subsided, he flips me over and rams into me from behind, one hand firmly gripping my hip, the other reaching out to grab my hair, pulling my head back.

"Fuck you look so good, your pussy taking me like you were just made for me." He releases my hair and moves his hand to my breast. "Put your hands on the headboard," he orders, and I comply quicker than I thought I would.

I grip the board and he rams that huge cock in and out, both hands on my hips. I feel myself building as he thrusts hard and harder. As my third orgasm of the night explodes, he groans out, "Fuck, Nora, you are so tight when you come. Your pussy feels so good clenching around my cock." And with that, I feel his release with a loud groan, and he whispers in my ear, "You are fucking perfect."

We fall to the bed still panting and he draws me close to his body, my back to his chest and his arms tightly wrapped around me. He nuzzles his head into my neck as we both try to catch our breath. That was amazing and I'm not ready for this to end just yet, so I stay where I am.

Chapter Eighteen

Aodhán

I held her so tight to my body, knowing that the instant I let go, she might leave. That is until I heard her gentle snores. She fell asleep in my arms–it won't be the last time, I grin to myself. I gently moved out of the bed trying not to wake her. Sitting back in the chair across from her, I watched her sleep all night.

I slipped out of the room quietly to grab coffee and breakfast, hoping I would be back before she awoke. When I returned to the room, she was sitting up in the bed trying to shield herself behind the bed sheets.

"No need to be shy this morning, réaltín álainn," I laugh. A slight smile threatens to edge off her mouth and I walk over to kiss her. Leaning down I run my fingers along her jaw before lifting her chin to bring her mouth right to mine. "Never feel like you need to hide from me." I press my lips ever so slightly to hers, separating her lips with my tongue and she gives me the access I crave. I could do this all day, but I draw back.

"There is coffee and food on the table." She shuffles off the bed with the sheet still wrapped around her and she grabs a cup of coffee while settling into the armchair.

"So, is this how you treat all your one-night stands?" she asks with a cheeky grin.

"What? No, Nora, this was not a one-night stand." How could she really believe that was all this was? Doesn't she realise how absolutely delicious she is? How could she possibly think I'm going to give her up after this?

"Oh, is that so? You're very presumptuous, aren't you," she smiles. "I don't even know your name Mr. Coffee Shop Guy." I laugh, there is the feisty little one I've been expecting.

"Coffee Shop Guy?" Wow, she's been thinking about me since that first encounter too.

"Well, what else was I going to call you? Stalker?" Guess I deserved that one.

"Aodhán. You can call me, Aodhán, I'm the man who had you quivering and praising God in my stead last night. What more do you want to know?" I can't really tell her anything about my line of work, but I know lying at this point won't end well for me further down the road. Maybe if I keep it mostly honest, perhaps, later it won't matter.

She is blushing, clearly at the thoughts of last night. "Okay, straight up bio points as a start. What age are you? Any family? Single, I hope?" she nervously chuckles.

That makes me laugh. "I'm 30. I have 2 brothers, Cormac and Riley, I'm the middle child, and yes I'm single–for now. Your turn."

She eyes me suspiciously "For now?"

I nod. "Depending on how this goes of course."

Her face turns bright red and this time it begins to reach down her throat and onto her chest.

"Hey, my eyes are up here"

"Yes, of course they are, and what beautiful eyes they are. It's still your turn, remember?' I retort, like I don't already know all of this.

"Fair's fair, I guess. I'm 28 and an only child. My parents died in a car accident ten years ago, I've pretty much been on my own since then, apart from my friends. I guess you know about them, right? Considering my invite had two plus ones, that's quite specific don't you think?. And I'm single as you are well aware, having crashed my last date."

Date? No, that was a minor inconvenience. Time for a topic change.

"What do you like to do for fun, Nora"

"As you have already discovered I love to read, and drink coffee, but I'm also a total chocoholic. If there was a job out there where I could just sit in a coffee shop eating chocolate cake and reading books, I'd be all over it. What about you, what do you like to do for fun, Aodhán?"

I knew I was going to love the way she spoke my name. I pause for a moment, running my eyes all over her body, before refocusing on her face. "You." Well, that certainly got her blushing all over again. "Let's do something fun today?"

"Erm that sounds nice, but honestly, I need to get going."

"You wouldn't be trying to get away from me, now, would you?"

"Definitely not. I mean, no, I... I... I need to get home to, um, feed my cats. They have already gone without their midnight feast after I didn't manage to make it home last night." She pulls her bottom lip so effortlessly between her teeth as she picks at her nails nervously.

"Okay, tell you what I'll take you home. You can feed the cats and while you are there you can pack a bag, and we can stow away here to enjoy the rest of the weekend." Flashing her a cheeky grin I know will get her.

She laughs and blushes at the same time.

"Got you. You want to say 'yes', so just say it." She hesitates so I move towards her. "Let me show you how much fun you are coming back to." I drop down between her legs, inhaling that delicious apple blossom and warm summer rain scent, I just can't get enough of, before worshipping her perfect pussy once again.

Chapter Nineteen

Nora

I'm a panting mess as the fuzzy feeling of my orgasm dissipates. Aodhán stands and grins, "To be continued," before stepping into the bathroom. I hear the sound of the shower running and I lean back in the chair running my fingers through my hair trying to convince myself all this is real.

Sitting forward, I look around the room for my phone and then remember I dropped everything at the front door. A smile forms on my face as I think of how we arrived here last night, and how Aodhán carried me to this very room. I'm still amazed at that. Given my size, I never thought I'd see the day I'd be carried like that. I wrap the bed sheet tight around me and head out of the room in search of the stairs.

I find them at the end of the hall, and I take in the beautiful surroundings. The staircase curves around and leads into the open hall at the bottom. I walk down holding on to the barrister as if it's the only thing keeping me from collapsing under the gravity of the situation I find myself in. Reaching the bottom, I see my dress and shoes in a pile by the door. Oops, guess we really did just about get inside.

Bending down, I grab my phone and message the girls to let them know I'm okay. We had previously discussed what would happen if my Coffee Shop Guy showed up, so they knew I was safe enough. At least, I'd convinced them I thought I'd be safe enough.

Finding the kitchen, I pour myself a glass of water. There was a lot of free champagne and I know that if I don't get hydrated soon, I'm going to have one hell of a hangover. As I turn from the sink, I notice the French doors leading into the garden. It is so beautiful here and peaceful.

Two arms wrap around me, and I jump slightly. "I hope you aren't trying to sneak away from me?"

"In a bed sheet? I doubt I'd get very far."

"I left some clothes on the bed for you, that way you don't have to do the walk of shame when we get to yours."

I turn to face him. "You really did think of everything didn't you?" I say as I pull him closer and kiss him. He runs his hand through my hair and his other arm pulls me closer still.

"If you keep this up, I'm going to drag you back to bed and those cats can starve. I've always been more of a dog person anyway." He groans as I step back.

"I won't be long."

Heading back upstairs to his room, I find the clothes on the bed. The underwear, jeans, jumper and even the trainers are all in my size. This man will never cease to amaze me. I jump into the shower for a quick wash before getting dressed and sticking my hair back in a ponytail. I wish I'd packed some makeup in my handbag. At least we are going straight to my place. I can fix myself up there.

I find Aodhán still in the same place I left him in the kitchen staring out to the garden. I decide to greet him in a similar fashion and wrap my arms around his waist. "A penny for your thoughts."

"I was just thinking about where I want to take you today."

"Is that so? And where would that be?"

"You will just have to wait and see," he says while turning around and cupping my face in his hands. "Are you ready to go?"

"I was born ready."

He leans in and kisses me gently before grasping my hand in his and leading me outside to the car.

Driving to my place, he keeps his hand on my thigh and keeps looking over at me as if he can't believe I'm here. As we pull up outside my building, he walks around and opens my door. I lead him up to my apartment and the cats greet me at the door, meowing louder than I've heard in a long time. I guess they are quite hungry.

I decide to test the water. "I'm going to grab my gear and you can feed the cats. The food is in the cupboard under the kitchen sink. You know where that is, right?" I say with a sly grin biting my lip.

He doesn't even try to disguise his surprise. "What? How?"

"That smell of yours is quite distinct and you mentioned my books, it wasn't exactly rocket science putting it all together."

His face is a pretty picture. *Got ya!* But then the cheekiest grin begins to grow. "Yeah ok, but I still got you interested though, right?"

"You're lucky you're good in bed, Mister." I shout as I flee down the hall to my room and I hear him laughing to himself.

Standing in my room, I add some clothes to my overnight bag. Wondering if this will just be one great weekend, and that's that. The intrigue and infatuation will wear off, right? I mean, I may be confident in myself, but I'm well aware of my fuller appearance, and that man is so chiselled and hot.

Catch yerself on Nora. There's no way I'm endgame for him.

Chapter Twenty

Aodhán

This cheeky little brat knew I was here. I guess I wasn't that great at 'stalking' her, or perhaps she was that good at noticing things. I shake my head in amazement as I reach the kitchen and sort the cats out with some food while they twirl in and out around my legs purring like little engines. I may have always been a dog person, but I hate to admit these cats are too damn cute.

I make my way into the living room while I wait for Nora. I grab a book from her bookshelf and settle on the couch to read a bit. Flicking through the book, I find the naughty part. Wow, this is pretty steamy. I am so taking this with me. For research purposes, obviously.

I'm so lost in the book that I don't hear Nora sneak up on me until she leans in and asks what I'm reading. Flustered, I jump up and it's my turn to blush. I feel like I've just been caught watching porn. "I... I..."

"Oh, cat got your tongue, big boy?"

Big boy? That was like a direct rush to my groin. I try to adjust myself without her noticing and I fail miserably as she laughs.

"So, where are we off to, then?" she asks with a little glint in her eyes.

I lean in to whisper gently in her ear and I notice the sudden hitch in her breathing. I can't believe I affect her as clearly as she affects me. "It's a surprise."

Her eyebrows furrow. "Is this the part where I find out you really are a serial killer who stalked, charmed and fucked me, and now you're going to kill me?"

I can't help but laugh. Whilst this did start out a bit stalkerish, my girl has a wicked imagination. "No, Nora. I have no intention of killing you. I'm going to take you to my favourite place in Belfast. I promise you will be safe. I just hope you like it as much as I do," I say with a wink.

She blushes and appears a little sheepish. "Ah, ok. Just checking."

I wrap my arms around her and pull her in close. Her cheek rests on my chest and she releases a sigh. I lean down and kiss the top of her head. "I told you, I'd never hurt you, and I won't. Are you good to go?"

She nods and I reach down to take her hand, leading her toward the door.

We leave her apartment and head back to the car. As before, I open her door and help her into the car.

"Are you always such a gentleman or are you just trying to impress me?"

"My mother raised me to be a perfect gentleman, and my brother would kill me if I was anything less than that," I say with a little sadness in my voice as I remember my mum. She nods as if she senses where my head went.

Deciding to take the scenic route, we drive through the streets of Belfast and up the Antrim Road to the top of Cavehill. I have always loved the view of Belfast from here. When we arrive, I help Nora out of the car and head to the boot. Pulling out a picnic basket and blanket I notice her staring at me with a smile on her face.

"Where did you get that?"

Her smile is infectious and I can't help but smile right back at her. "Oh, this little thing? I put this together while you were naked in my shower."

She blushes, obviously thinking back to this morning. "Any other talents I should be aware of, Mr. O'Neill?"

Fuck, the way she says my name sends a scorching pulse down my spine and directly to my cock. I look back with a grin. "Perhaps I'll show you later."

We walk down the trail and settle on the grass looking out across Belfast. It is beautiful on a sunny day, but even more so at nighttime when the whole city is lit up. I'm hoping she likes it here and is willing to see the day out. I would love to show her the view in the darkness.

The setting is perfect for a date. This may not have started conventionally, but I intend to be true to my mother's teaching, especially if Nora is to meet Mac. He will kick my arse if he thinks I've not treated her right.

Sitting down on the blanket, I open the basket and take out strawberries and chocolate, a selection of sandwiches, a cheese board with crackers and chutney, salted caramel Baileys popcorn, and a bottle of bubbles. Nora's eyes almost pop out of her head as she surveys the haul of food I packed into this picnic. She settles down on the blanket beside me.

"Aodhán, this is stunning. I love the view of the city from here, and you packed all my favourites. Should I waste my time and ask how you knew my favourites, specifically my weakness for Bailey's popcorn?" She eyes me intently, knowing full well that it is a wasted question.

"You got me. Although to be fair, you did post about your favourite foods for a picnic on the Gram, so it really wasn't that difficult to find out and I wanted to do something special today. I'm glad you like it." I lean across, pulling her by the chin, and kiss her ever so softly.

We sit there for hours chatting, eating, and watching the world go by. It's the most at peace I have felt in a long time. I never want this to end. But as the sun sets across the Lagan, the temperature starts to dip, and I notice her shiver.

Reaching behind me, I pull out a hoodie from the bottom of the basket and pass it over to her. She smiles as she puts it on. I notice from the corner of my eye, she closes her eyes and takes in a large breath. Man, am I glad it's a clean hoodie.

I pack up the remaining food into the basket and then pull her in close to keep her warm as we watch the sunset and admire the city in the dusk. Sitting between my legs, I wrap my arms around her and nestle into the nook of her neck.

We are still lost in conversation, which flows with an ease I have never experienced. It feels like we have known each other forever. As darkness begins to fall and visibility starts to disappear, it's time to pack up and leave. We head back to the car. Once inside, I blast the heat to warm her up and we sit there in the warmth looking out across the city at the twinkling lights.

"Aodhán, thank you for today, it has been magical." It's almost a whisper as she turns to face me. Looking directly into my eyes before dropping her gaze to my lips, she leans in and kisses me like I'm the very air she needs to breathe. I reciprocate, not able to get enough of her luscious lips.

It has been the perfect day. But now, it's time to take my girl home for a perfect night.

Chapter Twenty-One

Nora

I can't even begin to comprehend the effort and thought he put into this day. My favourite foods, the stunning location, and the view, yes him. I mean the view of Belfast wasn't half bad either, but I could have just stared at him all day. Maybe forever.

I don't know how long this will all last, but I've been through some shitty relationships and dates, I'm going to enjoy this while it does.

When we got back in the car, he held me so tightly, it almost felt like if he let go at that moment, I'd disappear. It was slightly unnerving. Do I really affect him as much as he affects me?

We sat like that for almost an hour until darkness properly descended and the full extent of the night view of Belfast became apparent. I thought it was beautiful with the sun shining, but the night view was something else. Hard to describe if you haven't seen it in person.

SEEN

I've seen many photographs, of course I have. It's the key place to get a photograph on the 11th night to capture the bonfires lit all across the city. So, every year it's the one plastered all over the media. It's hard to miss.

I always thought there was something beautiful about it. But here, today, with him, it felt magical. Intangible.

Driving back down the mountain, Aodhán reached over and held my hand, every so often lifting it to press gentle kisses across my knuckles as he looked at me. It was the sweetest thing I'd ever had happen to me. My stomach was doing summersaults, the good kind, not the kind that makes you queasy. The kind that makes you crave the person causing them.

We arrived back at Aodhán's house, which looked beautiful in the dark. Spotlights darted all around the fascia boards illuminating the house. The sprinklers in the garden were running and the lights on top of them glistened in the night, the transitioning colours making it look like a light show. Was it like this last night, or was I so wrapped up in him to even notice? Either way, it was spectacular and looked like something out of a fantasy novel.

Once again, Aodhán opened my door and took me by the hand leading me into the house. It had a real homely feel tonight, something else I must have missed in our haste last night.

I wander through the hall and into the lounge area when I hear Aodhán call me. Turning towards the sound of his voice, he appears at the entrance to the room with two glasses of wine. "Nightcap?" he says smiling.

"Well, now it would be rude not to, I suppose." I grin back at him, taking one of the glasses from him and then proceeding to sit on the sofa.

He walks towards the sideboard on the far left of the room and a few seconds later, music begins to flow through speakers that appear to be everywhere. I can't pinpoint a particular area that the music is coming from. It didn't really matter, but it was interesting.

Aodhán sits in the armchair across from me, sipping on his wine and just watching me. Feeling a little brave and seizing the moment before I lose my bottle, I drain the remaining wine from my glass and place it down on the table before walking towards him.

I can see a shift in his body, a little surprised at my move, but when my eyes meet his directly, I can see the desire dancing in them.

I lean forward with my two hands on the back of the chair on either side of his head and hold my face millimetres from his. Gazing down at his lips, I notice he is biting his bottom lip ever so slightly, so I push out my tongue and run it across his lips.

My eyes snap back to meet his, which were almost pure black. His pupils are completely blown. He grabbed me by my waist and pulled me down onto this lap so I am straddling him and using his right hand pulls my face towards him, crushing my lips with his in a frenzied kiss.

SEEN

I can feel the heat pulsating between my thighs and I try to move in an attempt to alleviate some of the pressure, but his left hand holds me tightly in place. His erect penis digs into me and his tongue continues to penetrate my mouth. When he finally releases his grip on my head and pulls back from the kiss, we were both panting.

He wraps both arms around me and stands up. If I wasn't so damn horny I might have been amazed at how this man can lift me so easily. He carries me out of the lounge and up the stairs to his bedroom, his eyes never leaving mine.

Stepping into the room, he gently sets me down on the bed. Leaning down over me, he forces me to look up at him by gripping my chin and pulling it up towards him.

He leans down and kisses me gently before dropping to his knees. He opens the laces on my trainers and removes each one. He reaches forward to the waistband of my trousers and looks back towards me, staring into my eyes, I finally realise what he is doing.

He is seeking permission before going any further. I nod and lift my bum slightly off the bed so he can slide my trousers and knickers off.

He places one hand on my stomach and pushes slightly, making me fall back onto the bed before he spreads my legs apart and starts to kiss up my inner leg, starting at my ankle up to my knee, then my thigh, stopping as he reaches my centre.

I can feel his breath on me and I try to sit up–*is something wrong*–but his hand, still placed on my stomach, holds me in place as his tongue darts out and licks me. The intensity drags a moan out of me, and while one hand balls into a fist between my teeth, the other runs through his hair, holding him in place, eagerly encouraging him to continue.

Tonight, everything was different from the night before. Still intense but with more time taken and less desperation. It was beautiful and afterward, I collapse onto the bed exhausted but exhilarated at the same time. We cuddle until late into the night. At some point, I fall asleep.

It truly was the perfect day. How long all this will last is anyone's guess but for now, I'm content to take everything I can.

Chapter Twenty-Two

Aodhán

Slowly opening my eyes, I notice that Nora is still curled around my body. Her head resting on my chest, her leg draped beautifully across mine and her arm curved over me, with her hand resting just below my face.

It has been a long time since I slept through the night, never mind sleeping this well. Perhaps it was all the fresh air yesterday, or something is changing.

I don't want to move and wake her. She looks so peaceful and beautiful as the sunlight peeks through the curtains and shines on her face.

I watch as she sleeps and gently lift my arm to stroke her hair. She starts to rouse and I hug her into my body. I don't want her to move away. "Good morning."

Smiling, she looks up at me, eyeing me somewhat suspiciously. "Good morning. Have you just been laying here watching me sleep?"

"Well, you are pretty fucking gorgeous when you are asleep and all curled up around me, so why wouldn't I just watch you?"

She shifts out of my hold, kisses me, and bounces out of the bed. Blowing me a kiss she heads towards the bathroom. I lie back and stare at the ceiling. I don't want this weekend to end. It has been a dream come true having her here all to myself, but she's going to want to get home today. If for no other reason than to feed her cats. But realistically I already know I'm falling for her.

Watching her for the last couple of weeks, and then really getting to know her, feel her, taste her… I'll never be able to give her up.

Moving out of the bed I grab my boxers and drag them on. Heading downstairs to the kitchen, I stick on the kettle and open the fridge.

With the music playing and the extractor fan buzzing away, I don't notice Nora arriving in the room until I feel her wrap her arms around me and her head pressing into my back.

"Hello, you, I was going to bring you breakfast in bed."

"If you keep this up I might not ever leave," she says with a cheeky grin. I know she doesn't really mean it, but my heart flips at the idea of her staying with me.

Turning towards her, I notice that she is draped in my T-shirt, tugging it forward just enough to allow me a little look down through the collar. I see she has nothing underneath it. "This looks good on you, especially as you appear to be naked under there."

"Well, I just threw it on as I was only intending to come find you. I can go back to bed and wait for you there if you want?"

Lifting her onto the kitchen counter, I place my hands on her face and kiss her. "I think I like the idea of you watching me make breakfast. Stay there and I'll get you a coffee."

Handing her a cup, I go back to finishing the food and then set the table. Once the food is served, I lift her off the counter and lead her to the table. Preempting her saying she needs to go home, I get in there first. "After breakfast, we should get ready and head to yours, I'm sure those cats of yours will need feeding. Although, I did get a little something to perhaps make that easier."

I retrieve the box from the cupboard and present it to her. She stares at me in bewilderment. "You bought me an automatic cat feeder?"

Starting to doubt that this was a good idea, I shifted nervously in my seat. "Erm... yeah. I thought it would allow you a little more freedom, you know, safe in the knowledge that they aren't about to go hungry."

Watching her ponder her response, I get the sense she has no idea what to say. Fuck, this was a stupid idea. "Sorry. Never mind, I can take it back."

"No, it's okay. I just never thought about getting one before. Thank you, this is really thoughtful." She stands and walks towards me, placing her hand on my face and kisses me. "I really appreciate this."

I pull her down onto my lap and cup her face, kissing her again. My phone starts buzzing on the counter and I try to ignore it. Nora motions to get up and I pull her back.

"Don't you need to get that?"

"I'm only focused on you. Whoever it is can wait."

The phone continues to buzz and she moves. "I'm going to get dressed, maybe you should see who it is."

As she begins to walk away, I flick my hand and land a little slap on her backside. She yelps, but smiles as she looks back. Lifting my phone, I've missed three calls from Mac. This can't be good. I call him back.

"Where's the fire?"

"What?"

"Mate, three calls, what's up?"

"What's up? I haven't heard from you since you bailed on Friday night, plus I forgot to grab beers. Can you get some on your way?"

Shit, Sunday dinner. O'Neill family tradition. After Mum died, Mac made sure that Riley and I still came over for dinner every Sunday. I guess it's his way of trying to keep her alive.

"Listen, Mac, I've actually got a lot on today, I don't think I'm going to make it."

"I don't care what you have on, you will be here at 3 pm. Do not make me track you down."

He's never let one of us miss, I don't really know why I thought he would today. Even when Riley is in training camp, he still has to come home. It's the reason he never goes away for training.

"Right, fine. I'll be there. You still make enough to feed a small army right?"

"Are you bringing someone home? Is it the girl from Friday night?" I can hear the excitement in his voice. I've never brought someone home, never wanted to, until now. Although I hadn't planned on doing it this soon, and I don't even know if she will agree.

"I'll be there at 3 pm." I hang up before he can say anything further. Will this be too soon for her? I guess there is only one way to find out.

Chapter Twenty-Three

Nora

I had just finished getting dressed when Aodhán walked into the room. He looks concerned, like he is nervous in himself. "Is everything ok?"

"Yeah, yeah, everything is fine." He runs his hand down his face. This is it. It's been a nice weekend, but it's time to go.

"Nora?"

I can sense the insecurity in his voice.

"Aodhán, it's ok. Just know that I've had a great time, but it has to end sometime, right?"

"What? No. No. The phone call was from my brother, Mac. We always have Sunday dinner together as a family. It's a tradition we carried on even after Mum was gone."

"Ah right, ok. Look I can grab a cab and be on my way."

"Nora, stop. I don't want you to go. No cab. I'm... I'm trying to ask if you want to... you know... maybe... come with me?"

SEEN

Did he just ask me to go to a family dinner? To meet his family? I can't help but just stare at him.

"You... you want me to meet your... your family?" I question, trying to determine if I have perhaps misunderstood.

"Yes. I would love you to meet my family. Look I know this is all new for us, but I'm not ready to let you go just yet, and I have to go. So what do you say? Will you come with me? Mac makes a pretty solid Sunday dinner."

I'm still in shock. I thought he was ready to call it a day, came to his senses, or whatever. Do I want to meet his family? I guess, it couldn't hurt, right?

"Erm... yeah, ok. We can swing by mine to sort the cats, right?"

His face lights up like a Christmas tree with a grin that would rival the Cheshire cat. "Yes? Yes, you're coming to dinner?"

Stepping forward, I put my hands on his chest and kiss him. "I'd love to." Excitement dances in him. He rushes to get ready while I head downstairs.

Heading out to the car, he is still wearing the grin like a kid in a sweet shop. Was he really nervous about asking me and so surprised when I said yes? I can't work him out right now, so I just smile at him as he opens the car door for me like the gentleman he's been all weekend.

The whole drive over to my place, Aodhán is quiet but the grin never leaves his face. Maybe this isn't a one-weekend kind of thing. Could this be something more? I've never had a serious relationship. I mean, I've had relationships, but not the meet-the-family kind of relationships. Could this be the beginning of one?

Arriving inside my apartment, it doesn't feel like I was just here yesterday. It feels like so much has happened in 24 hours, heck in the last 48 hours. Is this moving too fast? I start to doubt myself all over again as I head to my room. Flicking through the clothes in my wardrobe, I contemplate changing.

Aodhán appears at the doorway. "You are gorgeous, Nora, and you look great as you are. They are going to love you." He pulls me towards him and hugs me.

I close my eyes and take a deep breath, inhaling the scent of him. Normally, it elicits a different feeling, but right now it's very calming. I hope his family likes me. I want them to like me.

We stop at the off-licence to pick up some drinks before arriving at Aodhán's brother's house. It used to be his family home where his parents lived before Cormac took it over after their mother's death. I guess as the oldest he felt that he became head of the family. Perhaps, that's why he maintained their family traditions, even after all this time.

My nerves begin to fray the closer we get. What if they hate me? What will that mean for Aodhán and me? I mean, I know it's new and maybe it doesn't go anywhere anyway, but I'd hate it to be because I make a bad impression here today.

Aodhán opens my door, and I don't automatically move, so he steps towards me, taking both my hands in his. "Nora, are you ok?"

I nod, "I'm just nervous, I guess."

"Don't be nervous, réaltín álainn. I've got you. It's going to be grand. It's just dinner and then we can go if you want." The calm, soothing nature of his voice helps me to settle, and I take his hand, heading towards the front door.

Before we even get there, the door opens and a tall muscular, clean shaven, blonde haired man dashes out and heaves Aodhán into the air, spinning him around. "Where have you been hiding? They must be some great canaries in the Moy, brother."

I don't get it but Aodhán laughs. "Fuck's sake, Riles, put me down you eejit." Setting Aodhán back on the ground, the man who must be Riley, Aodhán's younger brother, walks towards me. I hold out my hand but he throws his arms around me and grips me in a strong bear hug.

"Riley, stop, you'll crush her," Aodhán sneers and he tries to pry me from Riley's grasp.

"Ah, relax aul boy, will ya? I'm just giving her the old O'Neill welcome. It's lovely to meet you, little lady," he tells me with a smile, and a side wink to Aodhán. I sense there is something I'm missing here.

"Nora. It's nice to meet you too, Riley." I feel Aodhán's hand on the small of my back as he guides me towards the front door and inside.

Chapter Twenty-Four

Aodhán

I've never brought a girl home. Hell, I don't usually keep them long enough to learn their names. The boys are loving this. They have already gleaned that Nora is important—how could they not, I guess.

Having survived Riley's crushing hug, I led Nora into the house and towards the kitchen where I knew Mac would be up to his elbows in making dinner. True enough the man who was always slightly smaller than me in stature, but older and more brutal in every other sense, was leaning over the stove tasting his famous gravy.

I clear my throat just loud enough to gain his attention. "How's it going, Mac?"

"Sweet mother of holy god, Aodhán O'Neill, on time for the first time in his life? Will wonders never cease?"

"That's not the only first today, Mac," Riley says with a stupid smirk on his face.

Here we go. Mac turns around to face me and his eyes dart to my side–to Nora. "I didn't realise we had a guest. I'm so sorry, Miss. My brothers were raised with better manners than this" he states, eyeing both Riley and me.

Suitably scolded, I turn to Nora. "Nora, this is my older brother, Cormac. Mac, this is Nora."

"Pleased to meet you, Cormac. I hope it's not an inconvenience for you, me being here?"

"Not at all, there is always plenty of food in our house," he replies with a smile for her and a side eye for me.

"Can I get you a drink? Dinner is almost ready."

"Thank you. I'll have a glass of wine if that's ok?"

"Of course. Riley, wine for the lovely Nora. Aodhán, you can set the table."

With food served and us all seated, the Spanish Inquisition begins with Mac asking where we met.

I interject before Nora has a chance to answer. "We met at Shadows on opening night"

Placing her cutlery on her plate, Nora replies, "Well..." Oh, this will be interesting indeed. "We actually met at the coffee shop in town a few weeks ago"

"Ah yes, I guess you could say we met a few weeks ago at the coffee shop, but were officially acquainted at the club."

Mac's eyebrow rose so far they could just about fall off his face. He finishes the food in his mouth and smiles. "So, you're Aodhán's VIP? Interesting."

She blushes and her cheeks turn the most fuckable shade of pink as she nervously bites down on her bottom lip. "Yeah, I guess that would be me."

Riley pipes up from across the table, "Right, and what do you do for a living, Nora?"

"I work for the government. Specifically the Justice Department."

Yup, that took the wind right out of them both for a second. Until the realisation that the timeline on our meeting was a little more suspect than they originally thought.

Mac is the first to voice it. "Do you work over at the courthouse by any chance?"

Surprised by the link, Nora is quite taken aback. "Erm... not technically. I work in the building next door, but under the same umbrella, you could say. How did you know?"

Fuck. They are both eyeing me like I just shit in their dinners. She didn't pick up on it, but I surely did. Then again, I guess I was watching for their reactions. This was always going to be an interesting introduction. I just didn't think they'd figure it all out so quickly.

"Lucky guess," Mac replies while staring directly at me.

The rest of the dinner conversation was more generic and less controversial, as far as my family were concerned anyway.

Riley took Nora out to the gardens where we always had our after-dinner drinks, while I helped Mac clean up the dishes, knowing full well I'd signed myself up for a full-on interrogation.

"Want to tell me exactly what is going on here, Aodhán? You've never brought anyone home and then today you bring a girl home that you met while on the run? Clue me in here."

Taking a deep breath, I tell him everything, from seeing her the day of my arraignment to the 'chance' meeting at the coffee shop and then the ball. I decide to omit the fact that I beat the shit out of some handsy bastard outside of the bar, or the time I followed her on that 'date'.

He listens intently, slightly nodding his head. "Ok, so what is it about this girl, then?"

I sigh, I haven't even worked that out yet. She is beautiful, intelligent and funny, but I still can't put my finger on why *her*. All I know is that the thought of not having her would be like telling me not to breathe. "I'm not sure, Mac. There is something about her that I'm not willing to give up."

"Does she know anything about us?"

"Not really. She knows about the club and the security of other bars, but not the rest and I'd like to keep it that way considering."

Nodding his head he replies, "Obviously."

Chapter Twenty-Five

Nora

Being an only child and losing my parents all those years ago, I'd forgotten what a real family dinner felt like. Watching the O'Neill brothers interact was lovely, but it made me a little sad.

Riley is super sweet. Though, it's easy to see how Aodhán and Cormac baby him. Not that he needs it. I reckon he'd give them both a run for their money.

Walking around the gardens after dinner, Riley was filling me in on his career, how he loves boxing, but also wants to give back to the community. His idea of opening his own gym, to help young boys and girls find an outlet and a safe space to belong, is inspirational.

"Oi, wee lad, stop hogging my girl."

Riley and I turn to see Aodhán walking down the path. He looks so good as he approaches. Leaning down from behind me, he gently lifts my chin and plants a kiss on my lips.

"I was beginning to think you'd run off and left me réaltín."

"Nope, not yet at least," I giggle and wink at Riley, who can't contain his laughter.

"Oh man, I reckon you've got your hands full with this one, Aodh."

"I certainly do," he replies with the cheesiest grin on his face. Like, I can't even with this man. "Right, beautiful, I think it's time we made tracks. Riley, thanks for looking after my girl and leaving me to the wolf, I won't forget it." He laughs as he drags Riley into a headlock and ruffles his hair.

"Get off, you bollocks. Took me ages to get that right for fuck's sake."

Releasing Riley, Aodhán turns towards me with a devilish look in his eye. "Time to go."

Heading back to the house Aodhán takes my hand and leads me through to the sitting room where Cormac is chilling out. "Mac, we are heading out. Catch you tomorrow, yeah?"

"Yeah, you better. We've loads on considering you've been MIA since opening night." His voice lightens up towards the end of his sentence as he turns and notices me. "Nora, it's been a pleasure. Take care of yourself and if this one gives you any bother, you tell me. I'll straighten him out."

Aodhán rolls his eyes and Riley laughs, but I pick up on the sincerity with which Cormac spoke. I can tell he is serious.

"I will, Cormac. Thank you for such a beautiful feed, it was unreal."

"Just trying to keep with my mother's tradition, you know." There is a sadness in his eyes I can't quite place.

"Right, no need for a long goodbye. We're off. Smell you later, muckers." Aodhán laughs and leads the way to the car.

He has the widest grin on his face as he opens my door before walking around and getting into the driver's side. "Your place or mine, réaltín álainn?"

"I've an early start in the morning so perhaps it's best if you just drop me off at mine."

"Your place it is," he replies not looking at me, but with that grin, I know that devilish look in his eyes is still evident.

The car journey is silent and every so often I catch him trying to grab a sneak look at me without me noticing. Still holding my hand, we pull up to my apartment block and true to form he hops out of the car and round to open my door. I could get used to this.

Walking me to the front door he smiles, "Home safe and sound, réaltín"

I still don't know what that means, but it sounds bloody delicious coming out of his mouth and I realise I don't want this to end just yet. I've known or believed that whilst this weekend has been amazing, it can't last. Can it? Fuck it, it's not over yet.

Sliding in the key in the lock and opening the door I turn back towards him and invite him in.

"Sorry, did you think I was leaving," he laughs, "Not a chance"

SEEN

Grabbing me by the waist and lifting me inside the apartment, he kicks the door closed. Caging me against the wall he lifts my arms above my head with one hand while the other caresses my face.

The desire is dancing in his eyes once again. My breath hitches and the warmth between my legs begins to radiate.

Closing the gap between us, his eyes on my mouth, his lips almost on mine. "Wild horses couldn't drag me away right now."

I can barely breathe as his lips crash into mine with a fierce need. I feel like he could just consume me and that would be the end of it.

I'd be lost in him forever.

Chapter Twenty-Six

Aodhán

Opening my eyes, I sit up in a momentary panic, forgetting where I am, until I look around the room. Nora's room. I look back towards the bed expecting her to be asleep beside me, but she's gone.

Throwing on my jeans, I make my way down the hall to the kitchen and sure enough there she is tapping away on a laptop. So engrossed that she hasn't even noticed me yet, as she continues to type one-handed and lift her cup to drink with the other.

I am once again mesmerised by her beauty. Her hair scooped up in a messy ponytail, and no makeup on. She is stunning. Wearing a pair of black joggers and a hoodie–this girl could literally wear a bin bag and I'll still want to rip it from her.

"Good morning, gorgeous."

Startled, she looks up from the laptop and smiles. "Good morning yourself, handsome, you looked so peaceful I didn't want to wake you."

"I'm surprised I didn't hear you. I'm normally a light sleeper."

"Guess you were just worn out," she says with a wriggle of her nose.

Walking towards her I wrap my arms around her shoulders and pull her back for a kiss. "Perhaps I was. Care to join me in the shower?"

"Unfortunately, no rest for the wicked. Tried to get the day off, but we were slaughtered, so no joy. You shower away, and I'll have coffee ready when you get out."

"Yes ma'am."

I could get used to this. Heading back down the hall to the bathroom I think about what she said about me looking peaceful. I am more relaxed here with her. It's a comfort and an ease I've not felt for the longest time. Checking my watch, I realise just how peaceful I must have been. 10 am. Mac is going to kill me.

Showered and changed, I make my way back to the kitchen where, as promised, she has coffee and toast ready for me.

"Cormac's been blowing up your phone, I guess you have to go," she says with a tinge of sadness in her voice.

"Yeah, I do but what time will you be finished up here?"

She eyes me with a hint of confusion. "I'm working until 5 pm."

"That works for me. I'll pick you up at 6.30 pm and we can grab dinner."

She stares at me barely blinking, but I can almost see the cogs rotating in her head. "You... you.... You mean you want to see me again?"

I move off the kitchen counter and make my way to her, her eyes never leaving my face, searching for an answer. I pick her up off the chair and into my arms.

"Oh, my réaltín álainn, I told you this was no one-night stand, nor is it a weekend fling either. I've been drawn to you from the moment I saw you, and with one taste of these beautiful lips, I was a goner. I have no intention of ever letting you go. In fact, if we didn't have work to do, I'd drag you back to my bed and never let you leave it again."

Holding her face, I lean in and kiss her, softer than before, but with so much feeling behind it. I don't know what pulls me to her, but I can't or won't give it up.

She looks up into my eyes, tears beginning to form in the corners as she nods and rests her head on my chest. I hold her there for a few moments until my bloody phone begins to buzz again.

She tries to break our hug, but I squeeze her in tight and kiss the top of her head. "Now that we've settled that, 6.30, yes?"

"I'll be ready," she says with a smile, even as a stray tear slides down her face. Reaching forward, I wipe it away with my thumb and lean in to kiss her one last time before leaving.

Reaching the car, I pull my phone from my pocket and call Mac. "Alright, big lad."

"Don't you 'big lad' me, where the fuck are you? Never mind, I can guess. Get to Shadows now, Emmett has news for us."

He didn't even give me a chance to respond before hanging up. This can't be good.

Chapter Twenty-Seven

Nora

I briefly hear the door closing and Aodhán is gone. The tears I'd been fighting back, fall freely down my face. For the first time in 3 days, I'm alone and the overwhelming emotions flood my brain.

I knew this moment would come, well I thought it would, but it's different than I imagined. It's not over. He wants to see me again. I wipe the tears from my face. They aren't sad tears, they are happy tears, with perhaps a little confusion kicked in for good measure.

I still don't understand how this man can be so feral for me, and maybe it will still all come crashing down. I've never been one to buy into the lines men feed women, but there was something so raw and sincere about the way he spoke about wanting me.

Could this be real? Who really knows? I'm just going to take each interaction as it comes, like I have all weekend. Take him at face value. He said he wanted me—I met his family for goodness sake. Surely that in itself would indicate this is not just some hookup.

I gather myself together and settle back into work, but in the back of my mind, I'm trying to decide what to wear and figure out where he might take me this evening.

As soon as lunchtime hits I waste no time in grabbing a quick shower. Standing in my room staring at my wardrobe, I pull out a long-sleeved summer maxi dress. Black but with silver detailing around the bust and waist area. I leave it on the hanger along with my denim jacket so I can get ready quickly once I log off from work. My ankle boots remain on the shoe rack, so I can grab them later too.

Moving to the dresser, I open my jewellery box and line up a long silver necklace with a blue crystal dahlia on the end to go with my dress. Simple hoop earrings and a knotted bracelet complete the set.

I throw on a t-shirt and shorts to keep me going until I have to get ready later, then run some curl cream through my hair, deciding to let my natural curls form for later too.

With not long left on my lunch break, I make a sandwich and a coffee and settle back into work. Only a few hours left and then I can beautify myself.

Eugh, I sound like a lovesick teenager. This is mental.

Chapter Twenty-Eight

Aodhán

Pulling up to Shadows I notice Mac and Emmett's cars outside. Bracing myself for the shitshow I'm expecting, I take a deep breath before exiting the car and heading to the back office.

I find them in Mac's office both staring at the computer. "Hope you two aren't checking out porn sites."

"It's about fucking time, come and check this out," Mac says with a touch of urgency in his voice.

I stroll around the desk and look over Mac's shoulder. Unsure of what I'm even looking at, I shrug my shoulders at Emmett.

"Don't you understand? Oscar was able to pick up footage from doorbell cameras that cover the shop on the Whiterock as well as the CCTV from the bar next door." Emmett shakes his head as he realises I still don't get it.

"The footage shows the car used in the robbery and who planted the crowbar, Aodh. We got the fucker who set you up," he says with a smirk as the realisation dawns on my face.

Staring at Emmett, "Who is it?" That is about all I can muster.

"Some low-rent little fucker in Murphy's crew, we have linked him with some of the higher-ups but we haven't gotten a name yet. However, this is proof that Murphy was involved."

I look back to the screen as the footage plays on a loop, staring at it, trying to place the wee bastard, but I can't.

"Has Oscar been able to track the car?"

"Yes, but it was found burnt out at the bottom of Divis, so it's no good to man or beast."

Mac leans back in his chair and starts to rub his temples like he's trying and failing to massage his brain to make the connection.

The door to the office flings open and Riley comes bouncing in, in a way only he could. He's like an overactive kid sometimes.

"Why wasn't I invited to the party?"

"Fuck sake Riley, I wish I had your energy," Mac quips at him before going on to explain.

Listening intently, Riley cocks his head and asks, "Let me have a look?"

"Fill your boots, wee lad."

"Aodh, you know who that is right?" he says, slapping me on the back expecting me to agree. The look on my face clearly indicates that I don't. "That's one of the wee pricks that kicked off at the fight. Do you remember that night we opened a separate book? He was a scrappy wee bastard. I'll never forget his face."

I shake my head as I begin to understand. "Fuck, so it is. How did I miss that?"

"Fuck if I know, lad. Sure he went for you after we locked up, swung a crowbar and all at you.'

Emmett, Mac and I are all still, staring at Riley, who continues to regal us with the story. I know what the other two are thinking; that's how my DNA ended up on the crowbar, but in all honesty, I don't remember that part.

"Sure, you ended up with a concussion and couldn't remember the hit the next day. Obviously, you still don't."

Emmett walks to my side, "Aodhán, they must have been planning this for a while. That was what, six months ago?"

"More like eight months," Riley retorts.

Running my hands over my face, I look to Emmett and ask if the peelers have this footage, he shakes his head and tells me he doesn't think so.

"Have Oscar hunt this little shit down. We need to find out if this was him getting back at me for that night, or if it's bigger? I'm not starting something with Murphy without more evidence."

"Are you sure you want to do this?" Emmett asks.

"Aodh, we could just hand this to the peelers and let them sort it out," Mac adds.

"If this turns out to be Murphy, we have to handle this on our own. Peelers have already tried to nail me. I'm not giving them another excuse."

Emmett motions to leave. "I'll keep you posted."

Mac nods and thanks him and so do I. "Right, now that's settled, let's get back to business. We have a shipment coming up from Dublin this afternoon. You need to get to the pick-up point."

"Mac, are you sure we want to keep up with this shit? Things are going well with the security contracts and with Shadows up and running now, don't you think we can just stop with that?"

"What and let that fucker Murphy take over, or worse some of the wee scumbags around here? No chance, this way we control all the shite in our area."

"Ok fine, we do it your way, boss." I practically spit out that last word. Mac hates being called the boss.

"Aodh, cut that shite out. I'm not your boss. We do this as a family, and right now we have to solidify what we have to survive."

"Ok, ok, just send me the pick-up address and I'll get it done."

"Thanks, lad."

Leaving his office, I shake my head again, this was not how I imagined my day going. I hate these shipments. I wish Mac would reconsider and stop with the drugs. I understand why he feels like we can't, but I really wish we could.

Chapter Twenty-Nine

Nora

Those last few hours of work felt like days. Like this day was never going to end. I guess it's all the excitement ahead of my next date with Aodhán.

Having finally finished up, getting ready was quick and easy with the prep I had completed at lunchtime. I dressed in the clothes I had laid out and set about freshening up my curls before starting in on my makeup.

I decided on a smokey eye with a hint of blue to tie in with my necklace. My mother always said that blue eyeshadow enhanced the blue in her eyes, so that's an added benefit too.

I fiddle about with trying to put fake eyelashes on for longer than I care to admit, to the point where I give up and settle for a heavy mascara.

One last look in the mirror and I'm happy. Not normally one to compliment myself, but I feel like I look good, so perhaps I do.

Pouring a glass of wine, I notice the time and realise I've managed to get ready in record time, less than half an hour. I giggle to myself; this is certainly new for me. I normally take forever, trying on different things and deciding I look awful.

Perhaps it was the preparation earlier, or maybe, having spent the weekend with a man who worshipped me has helped my confidence. Either way I'm taking this win.

Settling into the sofa with my wine, I grab a book from the pile on the floor and remind myself I need to get around to building those bookcases in the corner of the room.

I bought them months ago with the idea of setting myself up with a cosy corner where I could relax and read my books by the window.

Opening the book, I flick through to the last page I read and I pick up right where I left off, submerging myself into the story while I wait for Aodhán to arrive.

Suddenly I'm aware of banging on the front door and Aodhán shouting from outside. Rushing to the door I unlock it expecting him to be in some sort of trouble.

As soon as the door is open he bundles right into me, holding my face asking me if I'm ok, the panic on his face worries me and I begin to panic.

"Aodhán, what's wrong? What happened?"

Stepping back slightly to look closer at me, his shoulder drops and he lets out a sigh, "Nora, I was buzzing for ages, I tried calling and you didn't answer. Then when I finally got in, you wouldn't answer the door. I was so worried.'

My eyes darted back and forth across his face trying to read his emotions, panic entwined with relief.

"I'm sorry. I was reading and didn't hear any of it until you started banging and shouting. But look at me, I'm perfectly fine."

He takes a long look at all of me and then pulls me towards him, still cupping my face, he leans down and kisses me with urgency. It's like he's drowning and only my lips can save him. His hands reach around into my hair as he holds my head in place. Using his body weight, he moves me backwards until I'm pinned against the wall.

Breaking the kiss, we are both left panting. He places his forehead on mine, taking a deep breath and whispers, "I thought something had happened to you. I couldn't bear it when I could reach you."

The emotion dripping from every single word makes my heart ache. Bringing my hands up to his face I force him to look at me. "Hey, look at me, babe. I'm ok. Nothing happened, I'm ok."

His eyes widen and his lips crush into mine once more, but the kiss is more sensual this time. It feels more intense in many ways, but it's not as urgent as before.

Withdrawing from the kiss, he pulls me in tight against his chest and nuzzles his face into my neck. "Did you just call me 'babe'?"

I can feel him smiling as he speaks and it makes me laugh. "I guess I did. What are you going to do about it?" I ask as I pull back and raise my eyebrow at him.

"Well now, *babe*, I think our dinner plans have changed. I hope you like takeaway because we aren't leaving this apartment tonight."

I squeal as he lifts me and throws me over his shoulder while heading in the direction of my bedroom. My protests of 'put me down' don't get me anything but a swift slap on the backside and a boisterous laugh.

I have a feeling I'm going to be sore in the morning.

Chapter Thirty

Aodhán

Tonight didn't go exactly to plan and yet I couldn't be happier than I am right now. Lying naked in Nora's bed while she is curled around me, running her fingers across my chest.

Arriving to pick her up and the panic when I couldn't reach her was excruciating. The terrible scenarios I had concocted in my head tormented me until the moment she opened that door.

Even the cameras I'd installed were useless given the position she was in while reading. She was facing away from the camera while on the sofa. All I could see was her hair.

I couldn't contain myself once I finally got her in my arms. I knew right then and there that I was in trouble. But it was that smart mouth of hers that tipped me over the edge of the cliff.

Carrying her down the hall over my shoulder, like I'd completely claimed her as mine—which I have—was the best feeling I've felt in a long time, maybe ever.

SEEN

As I open my eyes, Nora begins to manoeuvre herself off me and I pull her closer. "Just where do you think you are going?"

Her laugh reminds me of the sweetest music, something I would happily die listening to. "I need the loo, if that's alright with you?" There goes that smart mouth again. I lean down and claim it before releasing her. As she reaches the door, she looks back towards me. "I seem to remember you mentioned takeaway before dragging me back here like a caveman?"

This woman will be the death of me and I'll gladly accept it.

Slipping into my boxers, I reach for my trousers to retrieve my phone. By the time she returns, the food has been ordered.

"Food will be here in thirty minutes."

She dives into the bed, pushing me backwards and then she climbs on top of me. "Mmh, thirty minutes you say. I wonder what we can do to pass the time."

Her smile is infectious. "I think I'm going to need to eat first, réaltín."

She gives me a little pretend huff, at least I hope it's a pretend one, as she flops down on the bed beside me. Turning to face me she smiles again. "You get the plates and I'll pour the drinks."

I can't help but watch her as she grabs my shirt and pulls it over her head. Standing up, it barely reaches her thighs. She slips on a pair of black lacy underwear, not dissimilar to the pair I liberated on my recon visit a few weeks ago. The thought brings a smile to my face.

Gathering the plates and cutlery, I lay them out on the table by the sofa and then sit back to watch her as she pours the drinks. Walking towards me, I'm in awe of her beauty, struck by the realisation of how lucky I feel to have found her.

My shining light. My réaltín álainn.

With drinks safely on the table, I grab her by the wrist, pulling her down onto my lap and she giggles. That is a sound I will never be done listening to.

"Tell me about this book you were reading earlier that had you so engrossed, that the world could have ended without you noticing."

Her eyes twinkle as she regals me with a brief synopsis of the book; demons, angels, hell and adorable hellhounds.

I pull her closer so that she is now sitting between my legs with her back to me. "Interesting, is it dirty?"

She blushes, and her face turns the most delicate colour of pink, as she simply nods.

Leaning back to look at the pile of books by the sofa, I ask "Which one is it? Perhaps I should give it a read."

"Oh my god, no way. You can't go reading my books."

"Why not? They are clearly intriguing enough to have you block out the rest of the world."

"Fine, on your head be it." She reaches down and lifts the book–Demon's Choice by Jasmine Wallace. Lifting out the bookmark, I begin to read the book aloud and she raises her hands to her face like she is trying to hide from me.

The door buzzer sounds and she jumps off the sofa like it's on fire. "Oh saved by the buzzer," she laughs as she rushes to the door to retrieve the food.

SEEN

Once the food hits the plates my stomach groans. Perhaps I was hungrier than I originally thought. Nora plates up the food and sinks back onto the sofa with her legs crossed.

We talk and laugh as we eat. She explains the story about the boxes in the corner and her plan for a reading cosy as she calls it.

I make a mental note to get right on that the next time she is out of the house. Nice little surprise for her I think.

What my girl wants, my girl gets.

Chapter Thirty-One

Nora

Lying on the sofa curled up around Aodhán, is just perfect. Not exactly how I thought this date night was going to go, but hey, best-laid plans and all that.

Looking up at him, his head draped over the edge of the sofa. I reach up to run my fingers along his jaw and down his neck to his chest. His cock twitches and I can feel it harden at my side.

It still amazes me how this man can be so feral for me. I love it. I continue to explore his chest with my fingers and tweak his nipple. He takes a sharp intake and his head snaps up to watch me. His bottom lip caught between his teeth, his eyes fixed firmly on his nipple in my fingertips.

I pinch it once more and his mouth opens a little as he gasps. I trail my fingers down his chest and run them across the waistband of his boxer shorts. Shimmying down the sofa, I kneel between his legs and begin to pull at his boxers. Without saying a word, he lifts his hips to allow me to remove them all together.

Tossing them to the side, I drop my face to his cock and lick him from base to tip. As my tongue circles his head, I raise my eyes to look directly at him. He watches me intently, still not speaking.

Staring straight into his eyes I take the head into my mouth and suck slightly. His eyes close, taking a deep breath and he releases a, "Fuuucccckkkk."

I release the head of his cock just for a second, then I lick the entire length of his shaft again, before taking him in my mouth. Moving my head up and down, taking a little more each time, until I feel it hit the back of my throat and I gag.

Tears stream down my face and I don't care. The noises coming from this gorgeous man, tell me I'm doing something right, and I love that I pull this reaction from him.

His hand flies to my head and he begins to lift his hips pushing his cock further into my mouth. I flick my eyes up to watch his face. His pupils are blown as he stares right back into my eyes. His mouth opens slightly as his breath shudders.

Suddenly, his grip on my hair tightens and he pulls my head back. "Fuck Nora, I'm too close. When I come, I want it to be inside you, with that pussy milking my cock for every last drop."

His words, and the intensity of his growl, send shivers down my spine and heat flares between my thighs as he pushes me back, and grabs my face before crushing my lips in a bruising kiss.

His hand slides slowly down my face and rests at the base of my throat in a firm grip. He trails his thumb up and down the side of my windpipe, releasing his grip slightly.

He releases my lips, which now feel sore and swollen, but I don't care. I will take everything this man has to give and more. He kisses the edge of my jaw and moves down my throat at a painstaking slow pace.

The inferno between my thighs is ready to explode. I reach to touch and he quickly grasps my hands above my head. He growls at me without even lifting his head. "Don't move or I will stop." His words vibrate through my throat and it draws a moan from me.

He leans back and smiles. I'm still wearing his shirt–I think he likes that. He reaches down and pulls the shirt over my head, but doesn't remove it fully. He uses it to tangle my arms above my head.

He continues to kiss down my throat, chest and then around my nipple. Sucking it into his mouth, dragging his teeth back and forth. Alternating between sucking and biting, as I feel myself teetering on the edge.

As he descends my body further, his grip on my hands loosens, however, I keep them right where he left them in fear of his earlier threat to stop if I move. My breath hitches as he reaches the top of my hip.

The anticipation is killing me and I roll my hips trying to angle them up towards him. The hand on my throat tightens, it's a warning shot, as he licks me, all the way back up to my nipples.

Removing his hand from my throat, he removes my knickers and throws my legs over his shoulder. He gives my clit a hard lick, throwing me over the edge I've been slipping towards. The orgasm rocks my body with an intensity I have never felt before, and he doesn't release my clit until the wave subsides.

As my breathing begins to settle, he grabs me and pulls me into his lap so I am straddling him, the tip of his cock lined up with my pussy. I'm aching for him to fill me, but he holds me in place, one hand on my bum, the other on my face.

The intensity on his face is matched only by the gruffness of his words. "I want you to fuck me, Nora. Take all of me and ride my cock." He plunges inside me with one hard thrust and then stops, allowing me time to adjust to this angle.

He takes my hands and places them on the edge of the sofa behind his head, pulling my body in closer. He buries his face in my boobs as I begin to move, rocking my hips back and forth. The friction on my clit becomes too much, so I try to pull back slightly.

He grips me tighter and forces me to continue moving, his face still buried. My orgasm begins to build and I feel my walls starting to grip him. He throws his head back and exclaims, "Fuck yes, Nora, ride that cock. Fuck me hard, baby."

Building the pace, my hips move faster and his fingers dig into my hips forcing the movement to increase further. I tighten my grip on the sofa and lean into him to get a better angle as I chase my orgasm, knowing he is right on the edge with me.

He slaps my ass cheek hard and I shatter. He continues to thrust as I ride the wave of ecstasy running through my body. The pulsing of my pussy sends him right over and he cums hard, I feel it shooting inside me as his movements begin to slow down.

Cupping my face, breathlessly he whispers, "Baby, you are so freaking amazing."

Chapter Thirty-Two

Aodhán

I couldn't sleep last night despite our antics. After the drama from a few days ago, Nora has not been out of my sight. Ok, so I know she wasn't in any real danger, but I still wasn't ready to be caught out like that again.

The few times I did leave–thanks to Cormac's incessant calling–I was able to keep an eye on her through the camera and Oscar was able to turn on the recording function so I could play back the footage. That did give me some peace of mind. It would have been useful the other day.

Today, though, she is going to the office to work, and I won't have eyes on her at all. I awoke early and just lay there watching her sleep. She is so fucking beautiful, and even more so, while lying in my arms.

When her alarm finally went off, I really didn't want to leave the bed, but sense prevailed. As she dressed and prepared herself for the day I made coffee.

Dropping her to work was surreal. I know she was only going to work, but I felt a sense of loss. This is a whole new feeling for me, and one I'm not entirely comfortable with.

Pulling away from her building, I just kept telling myself it was only a few hours and that became my mantra. My thoughts began to settle, that is until the phone rang and I saw Cormac's name. The man is relentless.

Answering, I shake my head and huff, "Do you ever sleep? I've had umpteen calls and texts from early on."

"Right so you knew I was looking for you and you didn't bother getting back to me?"

"I was busy."

"I know what your kind of busy is these days. How is the lovely Nora anyway?"

"Ah, Mac, she's amazing. I just dropped her off at work. I ... Never mind, what do you want anyway?"

"Just a few things, the next shipment is due at 3pm today. Don't be late this time. You know how the Dubs hate waiting about, and I need you to cover at Shadows on Friday and Saturday night. There's been a bit of trouble the last couple of nights and I could use all the muscle I can get."

"Fuck the Dubs, you know I hate dealing with them and their shite. Can't one of the lads do it this time?"

"Aodhán don't start again, you know it's necessary and no, one of the lads can't do the pick-up. They're a bunch of fucking trigger happy idiots at times. I trust that you'll get it done without starting a turf war. So just do the job and quit your yapping."

"Fine, I got it. Is that all?"

"Aye, I suppose. Don't forget about Shadows this weekend, don't let me down."

"When have I ever?" I hit the cancel call button before he has a chance to respond. It's not that I have let him down in the past, it's more that I want to highlight my annoyance at the whole situation.

I require some serious stress relief and I find myself driving to Riley's gym. It's been a while since I put in a good workout with him. Perhaps it will take the edge off my frustration for now.

Walking towards the gym, the smell smacks me in the face long before I make it to the door. Sweat and testosterone–it's oddly comforting.

It's not long before I'm in the ring with my wee mucker and he is knocking seven colours of shite out of me. Damn, either it's been too long, or Riley has gotten a hell of a lot better. My money's on a little from column A and a little from column B.

After a couple more rounds of him just beating on me, I throw in the towel and call it a day. Despite the hammering, I do feel better and ready for the rest of the day.

The exchange with the Dubliners goes as planned, with no issues just like Mac wanted. At least that will keep him off my back for a bit. Even with having to get the gear back to the stash house, I was still back in time to pick Nora up from work.

My favourite part of the day. Work is over and now she's mine.

Chapter Thirty-Three

Nora

Leaving the office, I spot Aodhán's car across the road exactly where he said it would be, but as I step forward through the double doors, arms wrap around my waist and pull me into a rock-hard chest.

For a moment, I am about to scream until I catch a whiff of my favourite smell. "You're lucky I didn't scream bloody murder, especially this close to the cop shop."

Throwing his head back, he lets out the loudest bellowing laugh I've ever heard from him. "Oh baby, don't you know the correct term is 'fire'? No one responds to help. But if you scream 'fire', the world and his mother will come running to your aid."

"Seriously? Fire?"

"Yup, it's a proven fact. Strangers don't want to get involved in other people's business, but they will always react to fire."

"Interesting, aren't you just full of random little nuggets of information."

"I'll have you know I happen to be very wise and knowledgeable, you cheeky mare."

I feign pure horror, stepping back slightly, and tossing my hand to my chest. "Did you just call me a horse?"

"What? No," his voice is slightly higher pitched than normal, then his head tilts and a smile cracks on his face, "but I do love to ride you so, perhaps it fits."

Excuse me.

"Aodhán O'Neill, you…" My words are abruptly consumed by his mouth on mine devouring them right from the tip of my tongue.

Breaking the kiss, he takes my hand and leads me towards his car. "Come on, we have plans, and whilst snogging the face off you is mighty fine, I'd rather we did away from here." His head twists back towards the building I had just left.

"Plans? Where are we going?" The possibilities flooding my mind, dates with him are like adventures and I can't wait for this one to begin.

"It's a surprise, but one I really hope you like."

I could already tell that this was going to be one to remember by the smug grin slapped across his face. I can't help but roll my eyes and return the grin as my heart dances in my chest.

Pulling into the car park on Dublin Road, I'm still in the dark as to where we are going. Aodhán helps me out of the car and takes me by the hand as we walk along the street.

Approaching the Trade Market, he lifts my hand to his mouth and kisses my palm. "This is just the first stop, I hope you are up for trying some cool food."

"I've always wanted to check this place out, but just never got around to it. Thank you so much for bringing me here."

We wander around the little stalls; the smells are delicious and I want to try everything. We stop and order some wings. Crispy wings smothered in hot buffalo sauce. My lips tingle with the heat.

Aodhán watches me like he wants to devour me–it makes my heart flutter. As I drop the bones into the bowl, he grabs my hand and licks the sauce dripping from my fingers. It is so sensual and intense, that I could jump him right now–well, if we weren't in such a public place.

I squeeze my thighs together trying to dull the tingling at my core to no avail. "Perhaps, we should take this home?"

"As much as I would love to take you home and continue this, I promise you'll enjoy this and then I'll take you." The innuendo gushing from his words sends heat rushing to my core.

Pulling myself together, we continue to walk around the market and choose some more food to sample. We picked up tacos and Filipino BBQ pork belly. The tacos were beautiful; crispy shells, spicy chicken, sweetcorn salsa and a smokey cheese–yummy.

The pork belly was out of this world. Sticky, meaty and a fruity ketchup that I just couldn't put my finger on. I had to go back and ask when curiosity got the better of me. Turns out it was their signature pineapple and banana ketchup. Not something I thought would work, but it was divine.

Our final stop is the sweet treat stand. Aodhán steps forward and orders gravy rings. My mind races trying to work out what the fuck are gravy rings. The confusion must have been written all over my face.

His eyes narrow as he focuses them directly on me. "You've never heard of gravy rings, have you?"

Shaking my head I reply, "No, can't say I have."

"You've heard of doughnuts right? Well, these are, I suppose, also known as doughnuts."

"Are you for real? So, where does the whole gravy ring come from, because that is so not what I would even conjure when I think of that."

He explains that it actually comes from the fact that in the olden days doughnuts were fried in a thick oil known as gravy. Apparently it stuck and in alot of places around Belfast these are known as gravy rings. *How is that despite living here for years I've never once heard of this?* He goes on to inform me that the types that aren't deep fried are what are known as ring doughnuts.

Even now that I know the history behind it, it will still never sit with me. Those are just doughnuts. Perfectly fried, crispy on the outside, fluffy on the inside and covered in sugar.

Finishing up our gravy rings, I can't help but reach forward and lick the remaining sugar from his lips. He pulls me closer for a kiss.

SEEN

"You are making this so hard, but we aren't done yet. One more stop and then you are all mine."

I can hardly wait.

Chapter Thirty-Four

Aodhán

This girl is so sexy, I almost lost it when she reached forward to lick my lips. It was so fucking hot. I had to adjust myself before standing up, or everyone around us was going to get a view of my erection.

A few deep breaths later and I'm good. I take her hand and lead her back onto the street. We walk hand in hand towards our next venue. A quaint little bookstore Riley advised that Nora would love.

Walking through the door, I watch her face light up. Her eyes close and she takes a deep breath, letting out the cutest little 'mmh'.

I've never been the type of person to look for bookstores, but her reaction tells me, I'm going to spend a lot of time learning all about them.

She dances around the store, like a kid in a candy store. Her excitement is infectious. Suddenly, she stops and stands still. It appears to be a reading area and when I get closer I realise why. It's almost exactly how she described the reading cosy she wants to create in her apartment.

She turns to face me and throws her arms around my waist, hugging me tight. "This place is gorgeous! I can't believe I've never been here before. Thank you for this."

"Oh, bringing you here was all for my pleasure, but it's not just a bookstore. Tonight there is an indie spotlight reading event."

Her eyes widen and she sucks her lips between her teeth as she tries to hold her excitement at bay. She throws her arms around me. "Thank you, thank you, thank you, best date ever."

"Only for you, réaltín álainn."

We join the rest of the crowd as the reading begins. Nora is lost in the event, while I'm lost in the emotions and expressions on her face. Right there and then, I make a silent vow to always strive to find ways to make her this happy.

I snigger to myself, as I realise the reading is about an obsessed man determined to do whatever it takes to get the woman he wants. My reaction is not lost on her, as she silently laughs and drops her head onto my shoulder.

When the reading ends, she mills around picking up different books, before starting to put them back. I can tell she is trying to choose which ones she wants, like she couldn't just have them all.

"Get them all, they're on me."

"No, I couldn't possibly."

"Yes, you can, and to be fair, it's a charitable action on my behalf anyway." Her face drops. "What I mean is, you have all these piles of books in your living room and there is this little, tiny one by the window, it looks so sad, so these will build it up so it's as big and strong as the rest."

That makes her laugh–phew, I thought I was in trouble for a moment. She gathers up the books she'd been lifting and putting down for the last twenty minutes. Grabbing one more, she heads for the till.

"Are you really sure about this?"

"I am. Now, can you get a move on and let's get out of here. You've had your fun now it's my turn."

Chapter Thirty-Five

Nora

It's rare for me to wake before Aodhán, but it's been happening more often in the last few days. Lying in his arms, I try to think about when it changed.

I remember back to our conversation a few nights ago, wrapped up in each other, he admitted that he preferred staying at mine, because his house felt so empty without me.

It was a raw and honest comment, but I think he rather regretted saying it, as he changed the subject quite quickly after that. I understood the sentiment, I felt it too.

I'd always been on my own but having him in my daily routine had become so comfortable. I don't even know how I'd begin to survive if he suddenly wasn't here anymore. My anxiety hit record levels at the thought of losing him. I tried so hard not to become dependent on his presence, and yet somehow it has snuck up on me.

What's worse it took Jenna pointing it out to me as I filled the girls in on how things were going;

My heart dropped as she squealed, "Nora, you do realise you love him, right?"

I tried to convince them or maybe convince myself. "Love, no I… I couldn't, I don't, I couldn't. It's too soon, it's a fling, I mean I enjoy his company. I'd miss him."

That's the moment I finally admitted it, to them and more importantly to myself. "Fuck I do. I love Aodhán. I'm in love with Aodhán."

They both laughed as tears streamed down my face, hugging me tighter than an anaconda with its prey. "Oh, hunny, don't cry," Emily said, wiping the tears away.

"What if he doesn't feel the same? Girls, I don't think I could bear it."

Emily piped up with her solution. "Let's throw a kitchen party, and Jenna and I can suss him out."

"Yes, absolutely. It's about time we met, officially, and anyway, Emily loves to host and it's been ages."

That had lifted my mood, and it was time the girls met him. If this was going to go somewhere, then he needed to know they were a huge part of my life. While we don't see each other, or even contact each other, all the time, our friendship is timeless and we are always there for each other.

Not to mention Emily makes a mean cocktail, and after a few of those, the tears of fear were replaced by tears of laughter as we caught up on everything from the past few weeks.

SEEN

We drank and we giggled. It was exactly what I needed. When their taxi arrived, the exhaustion and alcohol had started to kick in. I tried to clean up, but tiredness got the better of me.

Chapter Thirty-Six

Aodhán

The sun streams through the window and the warmth of it on my face drags me from my sleep. I knew I should have closed them last night. But arriving back after work, I found Nora on the sofa.

When I carried her to bed, she grabbed onto me and begged me not to leave, so I climbed in beside her clothes and all.

Turning to face her, I marvel at how peaceful she looks. I wonder, and not for the first time, how I came to find this amazing woman. Not only to find her, but to have her in my life.

Carefully, I sweep the hair back off her face and she lets out a groan. I imagine that hangover will hit pretty hard when she comes around. Thankfully, we had no plans for the day, so I cleaned up the mess from their girls' night. Given the amount of empty bottles, it's a good thing she's got nothing to do.

While the coffee brews, I grab orange juice, a bottle of water and painkillers, and leave them on the bedside table.

We spend the day chilling on her sofa. She reads her book, while I lay between her legs. She reads aloud to me and I close my eyes listening to her voice. I didn't even feel sleep take me.

"Aodhán…. Aodhán, sweetie, wake up"

"Huh? I… I'm awake."

"Food's here and Mac has been calling, but I didn't want to wake you."

I bounce up all disoriented and confused. I never sleep during the day. Lifting my phone, I call Mac while Nora plates up the food.

"It's about fucking time." His tone strained.

"Yeah, man, I'm sorry. I was sleeping."

"Likely story. Anyway, we have a problem. Our PR guy has bailed and we have a full VIP list for tonight's event. What the fuck are we going to?" His voice is hurried, with a hint of panic.

"What do you mean he's bailed?"

"Ah, Aodh, I don't know. Something about a dead dog. I didn't really hear anything after he wasn't showing up."

"Ok, calm down."

Nora nods at me as if to ask if everything is ok. I begin to explain as Mac shouts down the phone.

"Ask her if she would do it!" He's so loud she hears him and after a moment she nods. "Fuck it, it'll be a laugh."

Mac began spouting out requests so quickly I couldn't keep up, so I handed her the phone. She and Mac discuss the plans as she makes notes over the next half hour. I can see the excitement dancing in her. The subtle changes in her face between when she's listening intently, and when she offers suggestions he hasn't thought of, are evident. The curve of her lips flattens ever so slightly at first, and then her entire face illuminates. This woman never ceases to amaze me.

I can see the cogs turning in her head for the rest of the afternoon as she contemplates how the evening will do, continually jotting ideas and plans down with a sense of purpose and a hint of trepidation. So, it's not a surprise when the panic kicks in as we pull up to the club later.

"Hey, Nora, look at me. You are going to be amazing."

She leans forward in her seat and rests her head on the dashboard. Her knees bouncing up and down while she rubs one palm with the other hand. "'I just don't want to let you all down."

I lift her back gently and force her to face me, pulling her chin so her eyes meet mine. "Trust me, you couldn't if you tried, I promise. You are going to kill it in there. Now let's go and have some fun."

She was a total hit. Our social accounts have never had the traction we received tonight. The guests all loved her. She brought a real fun element to the festivities, and she even had her random question of the night, sparking some serious debate among the attendees. She told me after that it was her little ode to me. Gravy rings or Doughnuts? She's still not convinced even though the majority agreed on gravy rings. I guess it really comes down to what you've grown up with.

She absolutely smashed it. Not that I ever doubted her, not even for one second. Even Mac was buzzing, singing her praises, and that is not like him at all.

Chapter Thirty-Seven

Nora

Showing up at the O'Neill's traditional Sunday family dinner has become a delightful experience. This time, as soon as we arrived, Riley whipped Aodhán away, leaving me with Cormac.

We chatted about the success of the event the night before. He told me how impressed he was with my efforts, so much so that he offered me the job. Before I could explain I already had a job, he countered the offer by stating that it was purely for the big events, and that I could coordinate with the marketing team for the day-to-day promotions.

Whilst that did sound more doable for me, my insecurity around Aodhán began to factor in too.

"I really appreciate the offer and I'd love to, but what if things don't work with Aodhán? It would be really awkward."

Cormac shook his head and gave a little shrug of his shoulder. "I wouldn't worry about that. I have a feeling about you two."

His confidence in us took me a little by surprise. "Really?"

"Yeah, I do. You know I've never seen him like this before. He's changed so much the last few weeks and he's never brought a girl home. I don't think you have anything to worry about in that department."

As the conversation flowed during dinner, it astounded me how comfortable we all were in each other's company. It felt like I belonged here. It felt like I was home. It was comforting, and heartbreaking, all at the same time.

The grief and sadness surrounding my own family hit hard as we cleared up and I excused myself from the house, making my way out to the patio to take a breather.

I was so lost in thought, I didn't even hear Aodhán approach, until he was sitting beside me with his arms around me. "Talk to me, Nora. What's wrong?"

Twirling my necklace in my hand, a hard lump forms in my throat, tears beginning to flow down my face, and I struggle to even speak. He hugs me harder. "Baby, what's wrong? Did one of the boys say something?"

The fear of him thinking they had somehow upset me is enough to pull me around to muster a few words. "No," I sniffed. "No, of course not. They're great. They've been so welcoming and made me feel like part of the family."

He holds my face and forces me to look up at him. "You are part of this family, but surely that's something happy. Why are you crying?"

"This whole day has been so lovely, watching you guys all interacting and having fun with each other. It made me miss my family." I looked down at my necklace. The blue crystal dahlia gripped tightly in the palm of my hand. "It belonged to my mum. My father brought it for her when I was born. It's a blue dahlia, her favourite flower."

He reaches to touch the crystal as I continue to explain. "Dahlias don't naturally bloom in the colour blue; they have to be manufactured in a specific way to achieve the colour, so they are rare and expensive. My family didn't have a lot of money, but we had love, fun and happiness. My father knew she loved these flowers but couldn't afford to always buy them for her so he had this one specially made for her, so she would always have one."

The tears are streaming down my face and I'm sure I look like a mess. Instinctively, I try to cover my blotchy face. "I'm sorry, I'm just being an emotional mess over here right now."

Aodhán pulls my hand from my face, and lifts my chin forcing me to look directly at him. "Nora, from the first moment I saw you, I knew that I wanted to be with you. I wanted to make you laugh, to make you happy and to be there to wipe away your tears, just like this. I can't imagine what it's like to lose your family in the way you did, and feel like you are alone in the world. But baby girl, you're not alone anymore. You are mine and you are a part of this family now. Finding you was the greatest day of my life."

My heart swells listening to him as he pours out all his emotions. I can't find the words to respond. My eyes dart back and forth across his face trying to decipher what he's saying.

"Nora, you are my réaltín álainn. It means my beautiful little star. You are the shining light, guiding me in the darkness that is my life. Without you, I'm lost. I... I love you. I am so fucking in love with you, Nora."

My heart feels like it's about to burst right out of my chest. He loves me. He really does love me.

I throw my arms around his neck and hold on for dear life, as if letting go would wake me from this dream. "I love you too, Aodhán. I love you so much it hurts."

He scoops me up into his arms and twirls us around as he screams at the top of his voice. "She loves me too!"

Riley steps through the door with the widest grin on his face, with a bottle of bubbly in his hands. As the cork pops out with a loud bang he announces, "Well, it's about bloody time you two caught up with what the rest of us already knew."

As Riley starts to pour the drinks, I spot Cormac loitering behind him. He smiles and winks at me. "I told you, I had a feeling about you two."

I've never felt as happy as I do at this moment. How did I get so lucky?

Chapter Thirty-Eight

Aodhán

The last few days, since we both declared our love for each other, have been incredible. We have settled into our own wee bubble of domestic bliss.

With us both working during the day and then settling into cosy nights at home, it's the happiest I've ever been. I never thought I'd be the settling down kind of guy, but she is something else. For her, I'd do anything.

I had to leave super early this morning, and of course, she didn't make it easy for me. She kept pulling me back into the bed. I could have easily blown off the day and just spent it in bed, but unfortunately, I have a little problem I have to deal with today.

"I really gotta go, baby. I promise I'll be back this evening." She pulls the covers over her head and huffs.

"Fine, okay, I'll see you later," she whines as she peeks out from the side of the cover just enough to blow me a kiss. *She doesn't half make it hard to leave.*

Arriving at our biggest warehouse, normally reserved for our drug operation, Cormac is waiting outside leaning against his car. He nods in the direction of the main door. "We got the wee toe rag inside. Let's do this."

The main room of the warehouse is empty, but for a few tables by the wall and a single chair, which the boys have the scumbag tied to in the middle of the room. It looks like they took out their frustration on him as his face already looks battered and bruised, while his wrists are raw and bleeding from where he has struggled against the restraints.

Underneath the bruising and blood, I can't help but notice he looks like a little kid. He can't be more than 18 or 19. Dressed in a black tracksuit and white trainers, and that stupid skinhead look they are all sporting these days, makes him look like a proper wee smicker.

He pleads and begs to be let go, denying any knowledge of why we have taken him. Claiming he wasn't the one who tried to frame me. Refusing to admit that he was carrying out Murphy's orders. His pathetic words fall on deaf ears.

It's not until Jarly pulls a pair of pliers from his pocket, and begins to pull the wee fuckers fingernails out one by one and as the fourth one is extracted, he finally admits he was responsible for the robbery. His screams echo around the empty space.

It takes a few more before he cries out and states that, while he didn't know that dropping the crowbar would have the peelers pointing the finger at me, when it did he hoped that it meant they'd stop looking for him.

Once he starts talking, it all just comes flowing out of him through exhaustion. He swears his actions afterwards weren't thought out and planned. He is adamant that Murphy was not involved in any which way. He claims that the robbery was his idea and states he even got a hiding for it from members of his own crew.

He pleads for forgiveness and his life through the sobs and cries. He attempts to sell his sob story but no one is listening at this point. Sob stories never work. Everyone has a sob story if you poke hard enough.

He slumps over in the seat, completely done in, like he's got nothing left to give. It's hard to know for sure if he's telling the truth, but then again, perhaps it was my own bias thinking Murphy had a part to play in this.

Mac pulls me to the side and out of earshot of the rest of our crew. "Aodh, God help me but I think he's telling the truth. Even if he isn't, Murphy has had weeks to come at you again and he hasn't."

It's like he read my mind. "I know I was thinking the same. But I can't let that wee fucker away scot-free."

"Losing nearly all his finger nails is hardly scot-free but fine, if it makes you happy then the boys will give him another hiding and dump him."

"So be it." I walk back towards the wee scumbag. "If you ever cross my path again, I'll put a bullet in your head. Do you hear me?"

He nods. "Yes, sir."

"Ok boys, have a little fun before ditching him," I shout back as I exit the warehouse.

Mac is leaning against my car when I get outside. He straightens up as I approach. "I'll stick around and see that it gets done. We have another shipment coming in and I need you there to pick it up. We'll have this place cleared before you get back."

Lowering my head into my chest, I let out a frustrated exhale. It's pointless to object, as I have done many times, so I simply nod. "Yeah, I know and don't be late, right?"

Chapter Thirty-Nine

Nora

I've been floating around on cloud nine since Aodhán boldly declared his love for me. Looking back, I don't think I've ever experienced real love before. I know for certain I have never loved anyone, the way I love this man.

Heading out of the office for our routine lunchtime walk, I can't help but gush about him, so much so that I begin to imagine him everywhere I go. Well, not him specifically, but his car at least.

A black jeep with the same tinted windows as his, passed by us a couple of times as we walked our usual circuit. The first time I barely noticed it, but the second and third times, I noticed it was the same car, thanks to the number plate.

Initially, I put it down to them perhaps taking a wrong turn and had to drive around again. The one-way system within the city can feel more like a maze sometimes, especially with the never ending introduction of more bus lanes thanks to the new Gliders.

However, this particular car was then parked across the street when we returned to the building, and then again as I was leaving at the end of the day. I knew it wasn't Aodhán's by the plate, and he also knew I'd taken my own car today.

I tried to shake it off as just me being paranoid. Surely, there was a perfectly normal explanation. That was until I noticed it following behind me when I hit the motorway.

Again, I tried to reason with myself, but a sickening feeling descended when it took the same exit as me, and parked up at the end of my street. I couldn't get inside my apartment building quickly enough. The whole thing left me feeling very uneasy.

It played on my mind throughout the evening and I kept wandering over to the window checking if it was still there. After the third or fourth check, I noticed it was gone. When Aodhán picked up on my distracted mind during dinner, I couldn't bring myself to hide it from him. I felt like I needed to tell him, hoping he'd tell me I was being silly. But he didn't, instead he quizzed me hard on where I was when I saw the car, what time I saw it and any further details I could recall about it. It began to feel like a full interrogation.

I couldn't help the emotions from strangling me and tears began to stream down my face. Aodhán pulled me into his chest and hugged me so tight I thought he might crush me.

"Nora, baby, I'm so sorry. I didn't mean to upset you. Shit, I should have been there, I should have just driven you in and picked you up."

His voice hitches slightly with a hint of concern I've not heard from him before. I don't want him to worry, after all surely it was my mind playing tricks on me. At least, that's how I was going to play it off.

"Don't be silly. I'm a big girl and you can't be with me all the time. You have Shadows to run. You can't just abandon Cormac to do it all on his own to just be my personal bodyguard."

He holds me even tighter as he laughs so hard. "Baby, I would absolutely ditch him in a heartbeat to be your very own personal bodyguard, don't tempt me."

"No, you can't. He's already freaking out."

He eyes me suspiciously. "Has he been complaining to you?"

"What? No, I just know that he's been under a bit of pressure with the marketing team, and I imagine that running a new club is stressful. You need to be there for him and the business."

He drops his head and takes both my hands in his, raising them to his mouth, kissing both and growling. "Nora, I'd blow the whole place up if it meant keeping you safe and happy."

Those words and that sound send an instant heat between my legs. "Giving off some serious burn the world for me vibes. You keep this up and we won't make it through dessert."

His brow drops as stares at me with such intensity, before grabbing me by the waist and hoisting me over his shoulders.

SEEN

Walking towards the bedroom, he slaps my backside and proudly declares, "You are my dessert."

Chapter Forty

Aodhán

I've had Oscar trawling the traffic footage around the times Nora mentioned seeing the vehicle following her. I tried to rationalise to myself that it could be nothing.

That was until Oscar found the car and realised that the plates were fake. Unfortunately, the car disappeared from the coverage around the docks once darkness hit. The Harbour Police cameras are notoriously hard to hack and Oscar still hasn't been able to find a way around their security.

My mind has been racing trying to piece together what it all means. Does it relate to me and my business? Surely it cannot be a coincidence.

Mac certainly doesn't think so, immediately immobilising a security team to watch her around the clock. Whilst I was grateful for his quick thinking and action, I knew it would have consequences when it came to trying to have that conversation with Nora. She is bound to spot them and if I do tell her,

I'm going to have to deal with questions I'm not yet ready to answer.

First things first though, I have to find a way to convince her to come stay at the house. It's more secure, being in the arsehole of nowhere surrounded by trees, and it will be easier to hide the security team there than at her apartment. Hopefully, a few days at the house and then I'll be ready to deal with the fallout of them watching her while she's out of the house. If, or more precisely, when, she realises she's being watched again.

After yesterday, I made sure she let me do the driving today, and as I wait for her to finish work my heart begins to beat a little faster, knowing the first part of the planned changes have to be discussed.

I spot her coming through the security doors, backpack slung over her shoulder, just like that first day I laid eyes on her. She runs a hand through her hair as she looks around trying to see my car.

Once she does, her lips curl and a grin is splashed across her face as she walks towards the car. Stepping out of the driver's side, I walk around to greet her. Embracing her in my arms, I take a sharp inhale and her scent overwhelms my senses. "Hi beautiful, how was your day?"

"Busy, but I don't want to talk about it. Can we just go home?" Her eyebrows rise slightly, and her head tilts to the side, as she grins at me cheekily.

I can't help but laugh. "I'd truly love nothing more than to take you home. I've been thinking though, what about grabbing some stuff and the cats from the apartment and heading back to the house for a few days?"

Confusion floods her face, her lips flatten and her eyebrows rise as she watches me. "Really? How come?"

"I just figured we'd take a few days away from the world, and of course, the cats need to get used to the place sooner or later right?"

Her eyes roam across my face and her voice becomes shaky as if she's afraid to even say the words out loud. "Is that your way of asking me to move in with you?"

Move in? Her words catch me by surprise. That wasn't my initial intention, but as those words fall from those irresistible lips they stir something deep within my chest. I would love nothing more to have her living in *our* home. My cheeks hurt from the wide smile stretching across my face. I pull her towards me, holding her face in my hands. "Yes, I'm asking you to come home, baby. It's always been only a house to me, simple bricks and mortar, where I shower and sleep. But your presence there makes it a real home. Our home."

She pulls her lips between her teeth and her eyes begin to water. "Aodhán, I would love you to take me *home*." With a certain inflexion on the word home, that she says with a whisper, a single tear falls down her cheek.

Using my thumb, I wipe the tear away and pull her closer, crushing her lips with mine.

"Let's go home, Nora."

Chapter Forty-One

Nora

I still can't quite believe he asked me to move into this beautiful house with him. It's all happening so fast, and it feels so much more natural than anything else I've ever experienced before.

Even Sooty and Ghost are settling into their new home with an ease I was not expecting. They are loving life, scampering around the place like feline ladies of the manor.

Although, we had to do an emergency run for extra scratching posts to stop them from destroying the furniture those first few days. Aodhán took it like a champ. I thought for sure it would signify a step too far for him, but they seem to have won him over in a big way. Little madams.

He set up an entire office for me in one of the spare rooms, complete with little hammocks on the walls, and a climbing frame in the corner, for them to play and lounge in. However, despite all the soft comfy places for them to chill during the day, my keyboard still seems to be their favourite.

Domestic bliss descended on us nicely, and I have found that I don't miss my apartment at all. This house is absolutely beautiful, and the gardens are divine, with large trees lining the edge of the property. I've taken to spending my breaks from work on the patio, just watching the world go by–it is nature at its finest.

I'm sure Sooty and Ghost will agree once they finally get out to enjoy it. All the advice I've seen suggests four weeks is plenty of time to ensure they don't wander too far once they get out. Only a couple more weeks to go, although those two seem pretty comfortable being indoor cats for now. There is still a whole world inside for them to peruse.

Deciding to finish work earlier today was the best decision I'd made in a while. I found myself lounging in the swinging egg chair on the patio, wrapped up in a fluffy blanket, a mug of hot chocolate and my new book–LIORA: Lost in Heaven's Touch by Ava Rouge. I'd shifted slightly away from my current demon romance phase, and ventured into this one, which promised fantasy romance with angels.

It was the perfect way to unwind after a day of intense research and meetings. I didn't even notice the early autumn dip in temperature as the hours whizzed passed me. Well, not until the automatic lights kicked in when the natural light began to dim.

Looking around the garden in the fading light, with the leaves beginning to turn into those stunning autumnal colours reminded me of a fairytale. I guess, I do get my happily ever after, after all.

The serenity of the garden was broken when I heard Aodhán call my name from within the house. "I'm out on the patio," I called back.

Sliding the door back, my hunk of a man stood with a smile on his face like he was taking in the picture of me settled and comfortable in his home–our home.

Stepping forward, he leans down to greet me with a kiss. "As good as you look just chilling out here, you must be freezing. Come on, I'll run you a bath before dinner."

I pull myself out of the chair, which is easier than it sounds as it swings from side to side each time I move. By the time I've managed to get out of it and collect my things, Aodhán is back in the kitchen, beginning the preparation for dinner.

With the blanket still draped around my shoulders, I wrap my arms around him from behind. "How do you still smell so good even after a day's work?"

He holds my hands in his as he laughs. "I hit the gym after work to train with Riley, so I got cleaned up there." Turning around to face me, he cups my face. "You are freezing baby, good job I made your bath nice and hot. It is ready, and food should be done by the time you are finished."

"How did I get so lucky to find a good man like you?"

"Oh baby, I'm certainly not a good man, and anyway, I'm the lucky one. I assure you."

He smacks me on the backside as I head out of the kitchen. I can't help but giggle on my way to the bathroom. Stepping inside the room, it smells amazing, and the steam is permeating off the water. The bath is full of bubbles and surrounded by tea light candles. He even left me a glass of wine on the side. I could definitely love this man forever.

Chapter Forty-Two

Aodhán

It's been a couple of weeks since Nora mentioned the mysterious car, and so far the security team have not seen anything untoward since. Perhaps it was just a coincidence. Mac and I agreed to scale the protection detail back. It was only by pure blind luck that Nora hadn't cottoned on to their presence as yet anyway.

Things have settled down and it has been amazing turning that house into our home. I wasn't lying when I told her it was always just a house before she came into my life. It felt so dead inside, and now it feels like home.

The shift in temperature outside, along with the darker nights, has seen us lighting the fire in the living room most evenings, and it is now where I find the most peace. Cuddled up on the sofa in front of the red brick fireplace, Nora nestled between my legs, my arms wrapped around her as she reads one of her smutty books, and the cats curled in around us.

I never have imagined being this happy, and now I can't imagine this not being my life.

Tonight though, won't be one of those cosy nights we've become accustomed to, as we head to a party at her friend's house. I expect I'll be getting the third degree, given that this is the first official meeting. Emily, I think, will be easy enough to get along with, but from what Nora has said, Jenna will be the toughest one to crack.

Arriving at Emily's house, Nora, with her trademark strut, just walks straight in through the front door without knocking, like she owns the place. Not unlike how I do at Mac's, I guess. I suppose it's hardly surprising, the way she talks about these girls like they are family rather than friends.

She leads me down the hall, past the living room and right into the kitchen, where most people seem to be congregating. The rest of the party is out beyond the kitchen in the patio area, under the gazebo, where the music appears to be blaring from.

After the obligatory introductions to everyone, the atmosphere shifts from awkward to a party vibe and even I start to relax. Sitting back, watching Nora interact with her friends, I see a different side to her. The night of the masquerade ball, I was so focused on holding myself back to allow her to enjoy the night, I didn't fully appreciate their interactions.

I find myself blending into the background, just watching in awe, as she jokes and laughs with them. Every so often, she looks in my direction, almost checking to make sure I haven't disappeared. I'm not going anywhere.

SEEN

I was so lost in watching her flit around the party attendees, that I didn't even notice when her two best friends appeared at my side. "You really do love her, don't you?" Jenna questions.

Without hesitation, I instantly turned my head to look her dead in the eyes. "Absolutely."

"Good, but if you ever hurt her, I swear, I will hunt you down and you'll wish you were dead by the end." The look on Emily's face tells me she is deadly serious.

Looking down at her, I almost snort as I laugh. "Well, Nora did promise I'd be threatened by the end of the night, so we are certainly on track. Trust me, if I hurt her, I'll let you kill me."

That takes her by surprise initially, but then the two of them appear to soften towards me. I meant it. Nora is my whole world, and the thought of hurting her is devastating to me. I would never forgive myself.

The rest of the night is filled with fun and laughter. I can see why they are such good friends, and I appreciate that my girl has them in her life.

As the partygoers begin to disperse, there is only the core group left, and Emily sets about lighting the fire pit off to the side of the gazebo, as everyone enjoys the quiet hum of conversations.

I find myself in a chair beside the fire and in a state of contentment. How my life has changed over the last few months is incredible.

Nora joins me on the chair with a blanket she acquired, and she curls up on my lap resting her head on my shoulder. "I hope the girls didn't give you a hard time."

I stroke her face, pulling her chin so she is looking up at me. "Not hard enough, I reckon. Are you sure they are your friends?"

She giggles. "They are softies really, well until you cross them, Emily in particular. I think you passed the test with flying colours."

We sit there just watching the fire crackle for a while and the rest of the group start to leave.

"You ready to go home, baby?"

"Home. Mmh I love the way that word sounds. Yes, Aodhán, take me home."

Chapter Forty-Three

Nora

Waking up, I realise the bed is empty, but for a gorgeous red rose and a letter on the other pillow.

> Good morning beautiful,
>
> I'm sorry I had to nip out to run a few errands. I won't be long and yes, I still made you coffee. Check your bedside table. I'll be back before you know it.
>
> Love A x

I roll back over, and right enough, there on my bedside table sits a flask. Unscrewing the top off, I'm hit with the delicious decadent smell of coffee. That man thinks of everything.

Coffee poured, I snuggle back into bed and continue reading the last few chapters of my book.

By the time I finish the last chapter, Aodhán is standing by the door with breakfast in his hands. Freshly baked scones from the local bakery–raspberry and white chocolate, my favourite–and as he hands me the bag, I realise they are still warm too.

"If you keep bringing me food and coffee in bed, I'm never going to leave it."

"Don't tempt me," he growls as he runs his hand down his face. "Unfortunately, we have a big night at the club, so as much as I would love to keep you here, we will need to get going soon."

"What a shame," I reply, winking at him as I take a bite of the scone. Warm and deliciously tangy, but sweet. It's like heaven.

I finally drag myself out of bed and into the shower. As I lather the shampoo in my hair, the door slides across and Aodhán steps in. His presence fills the space and pushes me towards the wall. From behind me, he glides his hands up into my hair and begins to massage my head, before moving me under the running water to rinse me off.

I attempt to turn around, but he holds me in place with one hand, while grabbing the conditioner with the other. He massages it through my hair and then allows the water to run through his hands.

Still stopping me from turning, he begins to kiss my neck and my back arches into him. I try to grind against him, but he holds my waist firmly maintaining the distance between us.

SEEN

His left hand slides down my hips and around my body before reaching between my legs. He twirls his fingertips slightly around my clit. It feels so good. He pulls me closer and once again, I attempt to grind against him. This time he allows it. I can feel him hardening with each movement, as he presses his cock against my ass cheeks.

His fingers slide down further and into me painstakingly slowly at first. His kisses on my neck deepen as he begins to pick up the pace. I can feel myself building towards release, but then he bites my neck and withdraws his fingers.

He steps back taking the warmth that enveloped me away. "To be continued later."

"Argh, are you for real right now? I was so close," I huff and scream as he removes himself from the shower and wraps a towel around himself, before slinking out of the bathroom.

Right, ok. So that's the game we are playing today, is it? Well, we will see how he likes it. Time for me to have a little fun.

Getting out of the shower, I dry myself off and strut my frustrated backside into the bedroom, naked as the day I was born. I head for the closet and pick out a figure-hugging black sleek dress that accentuates my curves and boobs, neglecting to add any underwear. Let's see how he likes that.

Walking into the kitchen I grab his attention and twirl. "How do I look?"

His eyes bulge out of his head as he stalks towards me and pulls me tight to him. "Fucking gorgeous, but are you really wearing this to work? I wouldn't want to have to kill everyone attending for looking at you."

Jackpot. "Now, now, they may well look, but only you can touch."

"Damn straight. Anyone lays a finger on you, I might find myself up on murder charges." He runs his hands down my back and grabs my bum. His stare intensifies. "Are you going commando?"

Double jackpot. "Oh, did I forget to put any on? Well, too late now. We gotta go."

He growls into my neck. "You will be the death of me."

Ding, ding, ding, triple jackpot. And with that, I turn and head to the door. This is going to be so much fun. I'll teach him to leave me hanging.

Chapter Forty-Four

Aodhán

Fuck! I have never regretted anything as much in my life as I do now. Nora sits in the passenger seat, and now I am painfully aware of the long slit in the dress that I missed before we left the house.

Her hand runs up and down the edge of the material, and occasionally dips beneath the dress, to where I know that pretty little pussy is uncovered. I reach over and she slaps my hand away.

"Uh-uh, no touching. It's not later yet, is it?." She giggles and I almost swerve across the road. This is going to be a long fucking night.

We pull into the car park at the club and she doesn't even wait for me to open her door this time. She just hops out and scarpers inside. I can't help but shake my head and laugh a little. She is a feisty little minx. Wait until I get her home.

I spend most of the night with a hard-on, watching her prance about the club, grinding into me each time she passes and then skipping away laughing. She may be laughing now, but I'll get the last laugh when I finally get her home.

My attention is diverted when a commotion breaks out at the entrance. I radio for extra security to make their way to the front and Riley joins me to inspect. Two young fellas, I'd not seen before, had attempted to barge their way into the club wearing trainers when my men stopped them.

They obviously didn't get the memo about the dress code and started kicking off. It didn't take them too long to run for the hills as Riley and I approached.

"Sorry boss," one of the bouncers states while the others stand in silence.

"No bother, but no more issues tonight, please, boys." I just want to get through this night, take my girl home and fuck her like there's no tomorrow.

"Yes, boss," rings out like a perfectly timed choir making Riley and I both snigger.

Returning to the main room, Mac waves me over and hands me a piece of paper across the bar. "Your girl asked me to hand deliver this to you."

"Oh, she did, did she? And since when do you take orders from anyone," I sneer as I slap him on the back.

"Hey, I'm not messing with her, she's the boss around here these days," he quips with a wink.

> *I'm done playing...*
> *Come find me!*

I shout back as he walks away. "Any clues as to where she is?"

"Now that's called cheating, but I suppose you could do with a hint. She mentioned wanting to check out your office," he shouts back and nods in the direction of the front stairs.

Interesting.

Opening the door to my office, I see her sitting on my desk with her feet resting on my chair. As I step into the room, she spreads her legs and pulls back her dress showing off her naked pussy, which is glistening under the lights in the room.

I stalk across the room ready to pounce on her, but she stops me. She kicks her foot up onto my chest, the sharp heel digging into my skin as I try to lean forward. She tilts her head slightly, looking directly into my eyes, as she runs her tongue along her top lip. "You owe me a debt, Mr O'Neill, and it's time to pay up. Get on your knees!"

Before my brain can even engage to process or respond, I drop to my knees. My body instinctively knows what it wants and I bury my head between her legs. I pull her swollen clit into my mouth and suck hard. She wraps her legs around my head pulling me in further.

I graze my teeth across her and slide two fingers inside her soaking wet pussy. "Fuck yes!" she cries out. "More." I devour her like a man starved, and her walls begin to clench around my fingers. Her release is starting to build, and with all the sexual tension built up over the last few hours, I'm not sure I'm going to last, never mind her. I replace my fingers with my tongue and she explodes on my face. Her juices run down my chin as she pants on my desk.

Not letting her grab her breath, I pull her off the desk and into my chest. Spinning her around I push her so she is bent over the desk. With one hand on her back holding her in place, I open my belt with the other, and my trousers pool at my ankles. I release my cock from my boxers and ram it straight into her wet and ready pussy.

She gasps as I refuse to give her a minute to adjust to my girth. Pulling almost completely out and slamming straight back in. Fuck, she feels so good and so tight, it feels like she has me in a vice grip. Her ass bounces as my cock glides in and out, and I feel her beginning to squeeze against me. I reach around and pinch her clit hard, and she screams out my name as she cums.

The sublime sound sends me hurtling over the edge of the cliff as my own release spurts out, coating her as she milks me for every single drop.

I withdraw from her and she stands, turning back to face me. She smiles. Her face is flush and she is wearing the most amazing freshly fucked look. "That was fucking hot," she whimpers as she grabs me by the neck and pulls me down for a kiss.

We walk out of the office hand in hand, all cleaned up and ready to finish out the night. There isn't long to go and I can't wait to get my girl home for round two.

Once the lights come on at the end of the night, it doesn't take long to finally clear out the last of the stragglers, and we close the doors. Mac does the end-of-night checks and then it's home time.

As Mac locks up, Nora, Riley and I head outside to the car park. It's a clear night, not a single cloud in the sky and despite the autumn temperature drop it actually feels quite warm for this time of year.

We say our goodbyes, and Riley reminds Nora not to forget the book she promised to bring to dinner tomorrow. I drape my arm around my girl and turn back to shout something funny.

I didn't register the sound of the first loud, sharp bang, but what I didn't miss was the impact of the hit on my shoulder, which swung me, the force of which pulling Nora around in front of me. I just about hear the second, third and fourth bangs before we hit the ground.

My brain struggles to catch up to what is going on, high-pitched ringing begins to penetrate my eardrums, and I feel Nora collapse on top of me. I manoeuvre so my body is covering hers.

I hear Riley and Mac both shouting, their words indistinguishable. More shots are fired and then the deep roar of the acceleration of a motorbike rings loudly in my ears.

Mac rushes to me as I lay on the ground hugging Nora tight to me. My senses kick in and my shoulder radiates in pain, but as I lift her head to check she is ok, she doesn't respond.

It's then I see all the blood. Coating my hands, smeared all over my shirt, pooling on the ground and simmering in the moonlight.

"Fuuuuuuuck! Nora... baby... Talk to me. Nora, wake... up. Please... baby... I... I... I can't lose you."

Chapter Forty-Five

Aodhán

My heart is beating so fast, it feels like it's about to burst clear out of my chest. I can't catch my breath, and my lungs ache like they are on fire. My head is spinning, and I feel like I'm spiralling into a deep dark hole.

I cradle her head in my hands while Cormac keeps pressure on her wounds. Riley is on the phone. I can't make out what he is saying as he paces back and forth beside us.

"We need to get going. The doc is ready and his team is mobilising. They will be waiting on us when we get there."

"Thanks, Riley, now go start the jeep. Aodh, we have to move her into the car, the ambulance isn't going to get here on time."

I can't even find the words to ask where we are going. I'm sure I know the answer but my mind is racing at the thoughts of losing her. It's like I'm operating on a low-rent autopilot at this stage.

I shift my arms under her shoulders as Mac takes her legs, and we slide her into the back seat of my car. I climb in beside her and rest her head in my lap. She looks peaceful, like she does when she's asleep. Mac reaches in and forces my hands on her wounds and tells me to apply pressure.

"Hold here, Aodh, and don't let go. We will be there shortly. It's going to be okay, just keep the pressure." I don't think I've heard him speak so softly. If my head wasn't elsewhere I might find it unnerving.

Riley tears out of the car park and heads towards Causeway Medical. It's a private hospital. It works for us as we have most of the doctors on our payroll. It's not far from the club, but the journey feels agonisingly long.

The whole way there I can't take my eyes off her. My hands are pushing down on her stomach, essentially trying to keep the blood in her body. She's lost so much already. Too much.

Arriving at the hospital, we are met at the loading bay by Dr. Conway and his team. They pull Nora out of the car and onto a gurney, whisking her off through the double doors. I immediately attempt to follow when one of his team stops me.

It's at that moment I feel like I've just woken up. "You better get the fuck out of my way." I rage towards him.

Mac puts his arm across and stops me. "Aodh, let the doctors do their thing lad. There's nothing you can do for her right now. Plus, we need to get that shoulder looked at."

Shoulder? I look down at myself and all I can see is blood, hers and mine. In all the chaos I'd forgotten about my shoulder. The pain rips through me and I drop to the ground in a heap.

As I sit in the emergency room, I watch the doctor remove the bullet from my shoulder. The pain is excruciating, but I take every last bit of it. It's nothing compared to the pain in my heart.

It only takes a few stitches to close the wound, and he tells me there shouldn't be any long-term damage. I don't care about any of that. I just want her to be ok. She has to be ok.

The doctor bandages me up, puts my arm in a sling and attempts to give me pain relief, but I refuse. I don't deserve it. This is all my fault. I did this to her. I brought her into this world. The weight of the guilt is so heavy, it's unbearable.

I try to stand, but everything hits me all at once, and I drop back on the bed with a thud.

Mac walks back into the room. "Aodh, you doing ok?"

"What the fuck do you think? Where is she?" I snap.

"Yeah, about as well as I imagined, I guess. Doc wanted me to let you know they're taking her in for surgery. One of the bullets is lodged in her abdomen and they need to operate to get it out."

"One? How many were there?"

"Two. Doc said the other one was a through-and-through in her arm. He said the surgery could take a few hours."

I drag my hand over my face. This is a nightmare. "I... I feel so helpless."

"Maybe you should reconsider the offer of meds. She is going to need you when she wakes up. You might as well try to get some rest."

"I don't deserve any rest. Mac, I can't lose her, I just can't."

"I know, Aodh, and you won't." There is an edge to his voice. He's trying to reassure me, but the undercurrent of uncertainty is unmistakable.

God, I hope she makes it through. I don't want to imagine my life without her.

Chapter Forty-Six

Aodhán

When I open my eyes, daylight is streaming through the window. The light stings my eyes, and the memories of last night come barrelling back with a bang. I don't remember falling asleep, and I certainly don't feel rested. I attempt to move off the bed but the sharp pain in my shoulder causes me to cry out.

Riley jumps to my side and the doctor, who I recognise as the one who treated me last night, arrives at the bedside offering pain relief. This time, I'm only too happy to take it from him.

Riley steps forward as I motion to sit forward. He reaches to assist me off the bed. "She made it through the surgery, Aodh. Mac is with her in the ICU. She's not come round yet."

Leaning into him I growl, "Take me to her, now!" Fuck the pain I'm experiencing, I want to see her. I need to see her.

The doc attempts to get me into a wheelchair but I shrug him off and head straight out into the corridor. I've always hated the clinical smell of hospitals. It reminds me of when my father was going through his treatment, and then those weeks we practically moved in before he passed.

The last time a person I loved came in here, they didn't come home. I can't let that happen with her. She has to pull through. I can't lose her.

Walking into the ICU, I see Mac sitting beside her bed, but I don't even recognize her, hooked up to all the machines. The medicine bag hangs on a hook with the tube running down to a cannula in her hand. It looks like a monster across her delicate little hand. The oxygen mask obscures her face as the machine rhythmically beeps. It's too much to bear, and I sink to my knees at the end of her bed, tears streaming down my face.

Mac crouches down, pulls me to my feet and moves me to the chair to the right of bed. Shakily, I reach forward and take her hand. It feels warm within mine–she's still in there. "Baby... please... c-come... back... t-to... me." I can barely speak through the sobs. It is heart wrenching seeing her lying there.

Riley sits on the other side of the bed. "Don't worry, Aodh, she is one tough cookie. She's going to pull through just fine."

Dr. Conway gently raps on the door and steps into the room. "Aodhán, we were able to successfully remove the bullet. She did lose a lot of blood so we had to transfuse her, but thankfully, we don't believe there will be any long-lasting damage. She will need time to recover. It won't be an easy road."

Mac is the first to speak. "Thanks, Doc. Do you have any indication when she might wake up?"

"It's hard to say. Her body has been through a traumatic event, but all her vital signs are good, so that's positive. I'll check back in with you in a few hours."

The hours all roll into one another as the nurses come and go checking on her. Mac and Riley take turns trying to convince me to go home to rest, but there is no home without her.

They finally give up and accept I'm not leaving. "Aodh, Riley and I are going to head out for a bit. We will swing by the house and grab you some clothes and things. Is there anything in particular you need?"

I shake my head. "No, just make sure the cats are fed and ok, she won't forgive me if they starve. Not that I expect her to forgive me anyway."

"This wasn't your fault. You need to stop blaming yourself. We will find out who was behind this." Mac is right on one count, we will find them and I'll kill them. But it is my fault, and I will never forgive myself, even if by some miracle she does.

"Yeah, Aodh, Mac has already been on to Oscar and the boys. They are all over this."

"Thanks, lads. I appreciate it." I don't know what I'd do without the support of my brothers right now.

They pull me in for a hug before leaving and once they do I sink back into the chair, reaching forward to take her hand in mine.

"I'm so sorry, Nora," I whisper as I kiss her knuckles. I lay my head down on the bed with her hand resting on the side of my face, and I close my eyes.

I'm not sure if it was sleep that took me, but I fell into the darkness thinking of her touch.

Chapter Forty-Seven

Cormac

It was an agonising wait while Nora was in surgery. I'm not exactly the type of man to pray, I mean, I'm not sure anyone would even listen if I did. But I prayed to all the Gods that night that she would survive.

It's funny, the lads and I have been on our own since our father passed away a few years ago, and then she came into our lives. She's become the little sister I never had, and I can't bear the thought of losing her now.

Aodhán refers to her as his light in the darkness, and I think she brings a light into all our lives. I can't even begin to imagine the depths of darkness he will descend into if he were to lose her now.

She is going to have a lot of questions when she does wake up. I can only hope she is willing to listen, and accept who we are, because there is no hiding what our family is after this.

For now, the only thing I can focus on is finding out who was behind this and making sure they pay. No one, and I mean no one, hurts my family and gets away with it.

Jumping into the car, I can't help but turn my head to look in the back seat. Her blood is everywhere, staining the seats and the floor. I won't settle until I avenge this wrong.

"Riley, drop me at the club and then get this off to the cleaners. Aodh can't see this."

"She is going to be ok, isn't she? I was trying to be strong there for Aodh, but this is bad right?" The last part is almost a whisper as if he is trying to restrain his own emotions. He can't even look in my direction as he speaks.

His hands are wrapped so tightly around the steering wheel, I can see the whites of his knuckles. I sense the fighter in him itching to get out.

"I don't know, Riles. But if she isn't, the fucking world will burn."

Arriving at the club, the crew are already there. Jarly, my number two, meets me at the door. Placing his hand on my shoulder while asking, "Mac, how is she?" It's funny how quickly she fit into our lives and with such ease. She was an instant hit at the club.

"It was touch and go last night, but so far so good. She's still not woken up yet, so Aodh's a fucking mess. Tell me we have something, anything?"

His shoulders droop slightly. "Nothing concrete as yet but we put out the feelers and if anyone is talking, we will hear it."

"Anything from Oscar?"

"He's tracked the bike to the docks, but the coverage is shite down there considering we can't get into the Harbour Police system, so nothing further."

"The docks? That's where we lost the vehicle that was following her a few weeks ago. We need to know who is operating down there. This can't be a coincidence."

"On it, Mac."

Nodding to him, he motions to the rest of the group and they leave. I pour myself a large whiskey. The docks? For fuck's sake, I never should have pulled the security detail. This is my fault, I left her unprotected.

FUCK!

Chapter Forty-Eight

Riley

Driving up the narrow lane towards Aodh's house feels so weird. I don't think I've ever been here without him being home. I open the door carefully, remembering what he said about the cats, and there they are sitting on the bottom step of the stairs. I'm not sure they are fans of me, fleeing as I attempt to approach them.

Stepping into the kitchen, the little black one appears to be more skittish, still watching me from a distance. Whereas the little fluffy white one is twirling its way through my legs. I'm going to be covered in cat fur by the time I leave, aren't I?

With the cats sorted, fed and water changed, I head towards the bedroom to pick up some things–change of clothes, washbag, charger and the like. I doubt Aodh cares about any of this, but it's on us to look after him, like he has done for me many times in the past.

Leaving the bedroom, I notice the office space set up in the other room as I pass. Stepping in, I realise it still smells of her. Refreshing, goodness and comfort. God, I hope she will be okay. I've always been the youngest and my brothers still treat me like a child, but Nora never did. She treats me like an equal. I wish I could have protected her better.

I venture towards the bookcase in the corner, smiling to myself. She is never without a book. While she may not be up for reading straight away, I decide to bring some just in case. Perusing through the titles on the shelves, I pick up a few I like the look of. Reading has never been my forte, but these ones have intrigued me.

As I stuff them into the holdall, my phone begins to vibrate in my pocket. Dropping the bag and fishing the phone out with urgency just in case it's news of Nora, I realise it's Motor, my trainer. He got that nickname due to his real name, Cathal Carr. It's two fold really, Motorcar and CC like the engine. Well I think it's cool, and no I didn't come up with it–he's had it forever.

Hitting the answer button, and before I can even get it to my ear, I hear him roaring on the other end. "Where the fuck are you, kid? You're late. Do you think I've nothing better to do with my time than bum about here waiting for your sorry ass to show?"

Yip, he's pissed. "Boss, calm down, I..."

He cuts me off, perhaps calm down wasn't the greatest choice of phrase. "Calm down? Not on your life, boy. You get your fucking ass into this gym now. The new guy is here and ready to spar."

"What new guy? You know what it doesn't even matter. Aodh's girl is in the hospital. We had an incident last night. I'll not be in for a few days. I've got to be here for the family, and besides, if I start punching, I'll kill someone."

"Fuck's sake, kid, you could have led with that. I feel like a right aul bastard now."

"Nah, Boss, you didn't know. Don't worry about it. Who's the new guy?"

"Nevermind that now, we'll get him settled. Keep me posted. Don't be too long though, we want to get the next fight set up, and I don't want you to get ring rusty."

"Ring rusty? Listen, aul boy, I could quit for six months and still run rings around most of those wannabes in the division. I'll be ready!"

"Yeah, yeah, kid, take 'er easy and keep in touch."

"Cheers, Motor."

Gathering the last of the things on the list, I lock up and say goodbye to the cats–yes, I'm one of those people, stop judging–and I head back to the hospital.

Chapter Forty-Nine

Aodhán

Watching her chest rise and fall, while the monitors all beep in rhythm, is more excruciating than the pain radiating through my shoulder at the moment. The nurses continue their hourly check on Nora's vitals and try to comfort me with words like 'stable', and 'no change'. Yeah, no shit, Sherlock. It's not like I haven't been here.

Closing my eyes, I wonder again why she won't just wake up. I'd give everything just to gaze into those deep sapphire like pools she calls eyes and have her smile at me. Lifting her hand to my lips, I barely whisper, "Come back to me, baby, please."

Riley slides into the room carrying a holdall and drops it on the bed. "Bro, you look like shite. The doc said you can use the staff changing room to get cleaned up."

"I'm not leaving until she wakes up."

"Riiight, so you think that, when she finally wakes up she's not going to be raging, while you're sitting there looking like shite warmed up?" I lifted my head and my eyes bore into his. He bursts out laughing. "Wow, if looks could kill, I'd be dead right now. Just go get cleaned up. I'll stay with her and if anything changes, I'll get you straight away. Promise!"

Running my hand through my hair, I exhale loudly. "Fine, but straight away!"

Standing under the spray of the shower, the hot water flows as I prop myself up against the wall with my good arm. It reminds me of being in the shower with Nora yesterday. My chest aches at the memory and tears stream down my face. I'd not cried in years and yet in the past 24 hours I've cried more than I can ever remember.

I turn the heat up so the water is scalding against my skin, and I silently scold myself for ever leaving the house at all yesterday. Anger taking over the sadness, I step out of the shower and begin getting dressed, which I assure you is not easy with only one arm functioning.

Returning to Nora's room, the door is wide open and I see Riley sitting on the chair with his feet up on the bed, reading aloud. I recognise the cover, it's the book she was reading a few weeks ago.

I shuffle myself into the other chair and Riley doesn't even register my presence as he reads to her. Leaning my head back, I close my eyes and listen to his voice, which at least starts to drown out the consistent beeping I've been accustomed to over the last few hours.

"HOLY SHIT!" Riley's exclamation makes me jump, stumbling out of the chair and straight to the bed.

"Nora?"

"Sorry, bro," Riley whispers as he removes his feet from the bed and appears to be readjusting himself. "I was caught up in this book. Did you know it is pure filth?"

Shaking my head and, for the first time since last night, I feel myself laughing. "Yeah, just the way she likes them. Not sure you'd find one she owns that isn't."

He goes back to reading and I move my chair closer to the bed, laying my head down beside her hand. I just want to be close to her.

Closing my eyes again, I imagine the feel of her hand stroking my face and running her fingers through my hair. I feel myself drifting off and the sensation begins to feel so real.

Chapter Fifty

Nora

Vaguely aware where I am, I open my eyes. The light hurts them at first, making them water. I reach to wipe the tears away and agony pours through my body. Flashes of memories hit me all at once, laughing with Riley, leaving the club, intense pain, loud bangs, and then darkness.

As my senses begin to return, I hear Riley reading and see Aodhán with his head on the bed, my fingers running through his hair. It feels damp. As I attempt to move, the machines around me begin to beep louder and faster. Riley and Aodhán both jump at the same time. Aodhán grabs my hand, tears streaming down his face. "Oh thank god, you're awake. Riley, go get the Doctor."

"Aodhán, what's going on? What happened? Shit, why is your arm in a sling?"

So many questions swarming around my brain, my head begins to hurt.

SEEN

Before he can answer, the Doctor enters the room. "Ah, Miss Kavanagh, welcome back. How are you feeling?"

"Like I was hit by a freight train. What happened?"

The Doctor pauses and looks towards Aodhán, who nods in his direction. "Well, Miss Kavanagh, you were shot. Fortunately, one of the bullets went right through your left arm, but the other was lodged in your lower abdomen, so we needed to perform surgery. Everything went well, but you will be sore for a few weeks."

Shot. Bullets. Surgery. It's all just too much to get my head around and I feel my breathing becoming erratic. The Doctor moves towards me and places an oxygen mask over my face. It does help a little.

"We managed to get all the fragments out and we don't believe there will be any lasting damage, but you will need some physiotherapy once you are back up on your feet."

Still unable to form sentences, I just nod.

"Get some rest and we will check in on you again shortly." He motions for Aodhán to follow him as he leaves.

Riley leans in and hugs me. "You gave us quite a scare, kiddo."

My breathing returns to normal and I pull the mask down from my face. Riley sits back down and I spy my book. "Were you reading to me?"

Smiling, he replies, "I was indeed. This is some top notch smut right here. Where do I get some of that?"

"I'll hook you up when I get out of here. What happened, Riley?"

His face changes, becoming more sombre and he drops his head to his chest. "Maybe we should wait for Aodh."

"Riley, please just tell me," I plead, desperate to understand what is happening. How did Aodhán and I both get shot? The last thing I remember is laughing together with the three brothers as we left Shadows.

I listen as he describes the events from the night before. The motorcycle that appeared to come out of nowhere as we were leaving the club, the shots being fired, Aodhán's shoulder. The race to get to the hospital. It's all so crazy, it's unbelievable.

My mind races a million miles an hour trying to piece it all together. I have so many questions.

"Do the police know who it was?"

His face darkens this time and he reiterates that we should wait for Aodhán as he rises from beside me and leaves the room. I can sense I'm not going to get anything else from him. Something isn't quite right here.

Chapter Fifty-One

Aodhán

I follow Dr. Conway out into the hallway, impatient to get back to Nora. "What's going on, Doc?"

"Look, Aodhán, it's good news that she is awake, but we aren't out of the woods yet. She will need help and support to heal. We will need to keep her here for a few days for observation."

"Whatever she needs." Dr. C is the best there is and she deserves the best care, after everything.

In that moment I realise that she is going to be asking hard questions, and I can't see a way out of not giving her the answers she is seeking. I rest my head on the wall, preparing myself.

I feel a hand on my shoulder as Riley appears beside me. "Hey man, you ok?"

Standing back from the wall, I straighten myself. "Yeah, I'm good. How is she?"

"Asking a lot of questions. I've filled her in on what happened, but she wants to know if the police are involved. I'll leave you to that. I don't know how much you want to tell her. I'm going to let Mac know she's awake."

This is it then, I guess. Make or break. I've no idea how she is going to respond. I step towards the door and take a deep breath. Here goes nothing.

Her eyes dart across my face, searching for something. It is unsettling. I don't know if I can do this, until she reaches for my hand. "Are you doing ok?"

I can't believe, even laying in this bed, she is worried about me. "I'm so glad you are awake, baby, I was so worried. I thought I'd lost you."

"Nah, tough as old boots me." She hesitates. "Aodhán, what's going on? What aren't you telling me? When I asked Riley about the cops, he got quiet and said I needed to wait for you?"

My chest feels constricted and it's difficult to breathe. I attempt to speak but it's barely audible. "I... I... I'm so sorry, Nora. I never meant for any of this to happen. I'm sorry."

The look of confusion on her face, breaks me even further. "I don't understand. What do you mean you never meant for this?"

"It's my fault, I... I..."

She pulls away from me and the confusion in her face shifts to anger. "Your fault? How can it be your fault?"

The words refuse to form, and the longer I'm silent, avoiding her questions and eye contact, she sounds more irate.

SEEN

"You need to man up right now and tell me what is going on? We got shot in the middle of the night. How is this your fault?"

This is it. The words come pouring out of me like I'm back in the confession box as a kid. She listens intently just staring at me. Her face is a mystery as she hides all her emotions from me.

I start with the first day I saw her in that court house car park, how I was so inexplicably drawn to her, why I was there in the first place, the escape, tracking her down, watching her and engineering the meetings at the coffee shop. I remember her funny nickname *Coffee Shop Guy*.

I explained the history between my family and Murphy's. The kid responsible for my arrest. What my job actually is–the protection, the drugs, and yes, the club. Yet she still just stares at me, her head shifting from one side to the other at times as she listens intently. I'm not sure how much she understands or is even taking in. Her face remains emotionless.

I tell her what we know about the car that followed her and how it's possibly linked to this. That we think there may be a new crew in town, what Mac and Oscar are doing to find out who is responsible.

As I finish speaking, I search her face for any indication of what she is thinking, but I can't read her right now, and it is the most unsettling thing for me. I've never been so unsure of anything in my life before, and right now I have no inclination of where all of this leaves us right now.

"Nora? Please, please, just say something. Anything, baby. Just talk to me"

She purses her lips and her head begins to nod back and forth. Her eyes darken before she drops her face into her hands. She begins to massage her temples and then she begins to laugh. Shite, this is not good. Screaming, shouting, even crying I was somewhat prepared for, but laughing? That's terrifying.

"Wow, so you're some big shot drug dealer thug swanning about Belfast beating the shite out of people under the guise of protection, and you've got some sort of feud with a rival group that resulted in us both being shot? Oh, and you tracked me down, and put fucking cameras in my apartment? Did I miss anything, Aodhán? Is that even your real name? Because, I have no fucking clue who you are right now."

"Nora, please." I reach towards her and she recoils. I could feel my heart shatter at that moment.

"Don't you fucking dare touch me. I want you to leave."

"Baby, please, let's talk about this."

"LEAVE NOW!"

"Nora, please, I can't just leave. Please don't do this." The tears stream down my face as I beg her to let me stay, to talk this through. I can't lose her, I just can't.

"GET THE FUCK OUT, NOW!"

The door swings open and Mac bursts in. He lifts me from the chair. "Aodh, let's go, give her some space."

He bundles me towards the door. I look back over his shoulder, and can see she has rolled on her side away from me. I can't see her face, but I can hear the sobs and see her body shaking.

"I love you, Nora, I'm never giving up on us. Never."

SEEN

Mac strong arms me out into the corridor and closes the door behind us where I collapse in a heap on the floor. The pain of leaving is so unbearable, my chest feels like it's going to collapse in on itself with the weight of the loss. I won't give up, I can't. She is the light in my darkness, the dream to my nightmare. I can't do this without her.

Chapter Fifty-Two

Nora

Listening to him talk, explaining the details of everything that happened, my ears began ringing, my stomach clenched, and I just wanted to vomit. My chest tightened and I fought to hold back the anger and the tears. The sting of betrayal as he strips away everything I thought I knew about him.

I turned away from him after demanding he leave. As angry and hurt as I was, I didn't want to see him walk out that door. I wanted to wind the clock back to before, when we were happy, in love and I was blissfully unaware of the man I no longer recognise.

I don't know how long I laid there with my face soaked in tears, my lungs burning from struggling to breathe, and my heart shattered into tiny fragments that made it feel like it would never be whole again.

It wasn't until the nurse arrived to check on me, that I finally opened my eyes. The world looks so different, and yet, exactly the same. I had no idea what I was going to do now.

All I knew in that moment was pain, physical pain from my wounds, mental pain as my brain desperately tried to decipher what had happened, and emotional pain from the hurt and betrayal. But mostly, I was in pain because he was gone and I was now all alone.

I didn't catch the first couple of sentences she said to me as she checked me over. But her insistence that I needed to eat made my stomach lurch. I couldn't remember the last time I'd eaten, and I didn't think I'd be able to keep it down if I tried now.

"Can I just get a coffee, please? I'm not ready for food."

"Oh hunny, if you don't eat we can't give your meds. How about even trying some toast?"

"Yeah, ok. Thank you." I resigned myself to the fact that if I didn't at least try, this pain wasn't going to ease. "Sorry, do you happen to know if my phone is here? I couldn't find it in the locker."

"Yes, Mr O'Neill left a bag for you. I'll bring it in now."

Opening the bag, the first thing that hits me is the smell. It smells like him, and that triggers another round of tears, as I hoke through the bag and find my phone. Turning it on, it beeps like a bitch, so many notifications. I opened the group chat messaging the only people in my life I can ever rely upon.

> **ME:**
> I'm in the hospital. I need you.

> **Emily:**
> OMG Nora what happened? Are you ok?

> **Me:**
> Yes and No. I'll explain when you get here.

> **Jenna:**
> We will be there asap.

True to form 20 minutes later my two best friends burst into my room and race to my bedside. I spend the next few hours telling them everything that has happened and answering the questions that I can. It's a lot for them to take in, sure. I haven't even gotten my head around most of it.

We hug, we cry and eventually there is even some laughing, although it hurts like hell to laugh, but somehow that makes me laugh even more. It's the absurdity of the whole situation.

Over the following few days, the girls take turns in coming to visit and even Riley drops in a couple of times. He doesn't mention Aodhán, and neither do I, as much as I ache to know if he's ok.

We chat about books and how his training is going. He fills me in on the new guy at the gym, Scotty. Riley talks like he hates him, but there is something deeper behind what he's saying, and there is a certain twinkle in his eyes as he talks about him. I have a feeling about them but I decide not to voice it. He will have to work that out on his own, and let's be honest, I'm not exactly one to comment on other people's lives right now. My own being a complete shit show.

Riley did agree to help the girls move all my stuff back to my apartment. I could sense he wanted to say something when I asked, but he is trying so hard not to get caught between Aodhán and I. The pain was etched on his face. This isn't easy for any of us, it's like we've all lost something here.

Spending time with Riley makes me miss those Sunday Dinners at Mac's house. I really felt like I was part of the family, even though it hadn't been that long. The hurt I feel isn't just losing what Aodhán and I had, but I feel like I've lost my family all over again.

Chapter Fifty-Three

Aodhán

Leaving the hospital that day, was by far the hardest thing I've ever had to do. It felt like my heart had been ripped from my chest. I tried to see her the first couple of days, but she refused to see me, and the girls weren't exactly thrilled to see my face when I showed up. I genuinely think Emily would have killed me right there, and I'm pretty sure I would have let her. Living without Nora isn't living at all.

I'm glad she has them in her corner. It would kill me if she was all alone because of what I had done. She's even allowed Riley to visit. That almost wrecked me, knowing that my baby brother could see her and I couldn't. But it gave me hope. She was still willing to be around him, even knowing what we do. Yes, Riley isn't as involved as me, but still it tells me that it's my betrayal that's keeping her away, rather than who I really am.

I have tried to keep myself busy, but every waking moment is filled with thoughts of her. Her beautiful smile, her infectious laugh and her feistiness. I miss everything about her. Even sleep is no respite, for when it does come, it brings vivid nightmares of that night, and the look of anger and hurt on her face as she screamed at me to leave.

Mac continues to work on who was behind the shooting, and in the meantime, we have maintained a high level of security around the hospital. She may not want anything to do with me right now, but I will make damn sure she stays safe. Most days, I just sit outside watching people enter and leave. It's the closest I can get to her just now.

The doctors have said she is progressing well and starting to heal, physically anyway. She's telling the doctors she's fine, but I know that the only people she will be sharing how she really feels with, aren't willing to speak to me right now.

When Riley called to say she wanted all her stuff moved back to her apartment, it felt like the fragile pieces of my broken heart shattered all over again. He offered to come and pack it all up, but I didn't want anyone, not even him, touching her things.

Packing her clothes away, it amazes me how much I can still smell her sweet scent on them, and the memories of our time here flood my mind like a tidal wave threatening to drown me in my sorrow. Leaving the hospital that day, I swore I wouldn't give up, and I won't. I can't.

Riley came with me to return everything to her apartment, including Sooty and Ghost. Those little terrors have kept me sane the last few days. The routine of having to feed them and keep them alive has in some way kept me alive too. They had even taken to sleeping in the bed with me, not that I did much sleeping. More so, tossing and turning. But they have been a comfort, curling in around my legs, and snuggling in tight. Somehow, they helped me feel like a part of her was still here with me.

Her apartment feels oddly empty. It still contained all her furniture, as we hadn't fully got her moved into the house, but it feels devoid of her. Riley starts unloading the boxes and gets the cats settled back in.

We unpack most of her things and place them back where they were supposed to be. Opening one of the boxes, I realise that she never got her bookcase set up here, nor the little cosy corner she talked about. I hate the idea of her moving back here, but if she is adamant that's what she wants for now, then I'll make it the best place possible for her.

I promised I wouldn't give up. I'm not. I'll never give up.

Chapter Fifty-Four

Nora

After almost 2 weeks, the day has come when I finally get to go home. Well, back to my apartment. I'm not sure it will feel like home now, but at least it will feel better than being stuck here.

Emily and Jenna arrive to pick me up, and I am more than ready to get out of here. The doctor insists I take a wheelchair to the front door, even though I'm perfectly capable of walking. Yes, it gets tiring, but I can walk just fine. Reluctantly, I give in and agree.

Emily carries my bag while Jenna pushes me in the wheelchair. Zooming down the corridor swerving from side to side, to the point where we almost collide with a doctor as he turns the corner. I burst out laughing and immediately, my stomach begins to hurt. "You're not meant to make me laugh, for goodness sake."

The two of them are bent over giggling like a couple of school girls. Gathering themselves together, we make it to the front door, and I am ready to get out of this chair, and this hospital. Jenna helps me into the backseat of the car and then slides in beside me.

She squeezes my hand ever so gently and mouths, "Are you ok?"

I shrug my shoulders. Truthfully, I don't know. It all still feels so surreal. I fell so hard and so fast and now he's gone. Sure, I may have sent him away, but he's still gone, and now I don't know what I'm supposed to do or feel.

The girls are aware of everything, and have been so supportive throughout this entire ordeal. Emily is still ready to kill him on sight. Jenna hugs me in the car, and as we approach my apartment, I begin to feel overwhelmed. Being in the hospital and refusing to see him or accept contact from him was one thing, but going back there feels harder. This bubble I've been hiding in, is about to burst and I'm not ready for it.

We pull up to my apartment building and Jenna helps me get out of the car. The pain in my stomach is immense when I move too much. They both put their arms around me, helping me up the stairs and through the front door.

Walking back into the apartment I left behind only weeks ago feels different. I used to love this place. It was the first thing I ever owned that was just mine. I worked so hard for it and I earned it all on my own. It had been my home before him. Now, it just felt like I was entering a stranger's apartment.

I'd asked the girls and Riley to help move my stuff back here, so at least I wouldn't have to worry about that. Heading towards the kitchen slash living room area, I was hoping that they'd unpacked it all too. I wasn't sure I was fit enough to do that by myself.

As I look around the room, my heart just stops.

My eyes are focused on the corner of the room, where there is now a full bookcase spanning the length of the wall. In front of it sits a similar swinging egg chair to the one at Aodhán's, with fluffy cushions and a blanket folded up on it. The bookcase is filled with all my books and even from here, I can see new ones have been added. But it is the vase on the windowsill that draws my attention. A large bouquet of blue dahlias.

Turning to the girls, they both shrug their shoulders.

"Don't look at us. We had nothing to do with this. He wouldn't take no for an answer."

Lifting one of the dahlias up to my face, I can't stop the swelling in my heart and the tears from tripping down my face. He remembered. I miss him. I can't believe he did all this. It was set up exactly like I described that night, apart from the egg chair, but then I had gushed that much about the one on his patio, I guess he thought I'd appreciate it better. I really did.

I slump into the sofa as Emily brings a tray of cocktails and ice cream. Jenna cuddles me as I drink and cry. She is always the voice of reason. "Have you really not even talked to him yet?"

I shake my head, unable to access the ability to even say the word 'no'.

"Maybe you should. Even if it is only to just acknowledge all of this?"

"Maybe." Is all I can muster as the tears refuse to stop.

We spend the next few hours just chatting, drinking cocktails and watching the trashiest of TV shows. Every so often my eyes would drift to my cosy corner and the tears would fall again. My emotions are feeling more out of whack than they ever have before.

Saying goodbye to the girls was difficult, but I needed some time to myself. I'm still trying to get my head around everything that has happened. The confusion in my mind still overwhelms me. I am filled with anger and hurt, but buried beneath all of that is a love I can't switch off, try as I might.

Climbing into bed, I bury my face into the pillow searching for a hint of him I know I will never find in these brand new sheets. Thinking back to our last night together, I feel the tears welling in my eyes threatening to fall.

No! I can't cry anymore.

Reaching for my phone, I begin to read through the messages I've been avoiding. There are dozens; *I love you... I'm sorry... I miss you... Please, just talk to me.* But it's the last one that hits me the hardest.

> Aodhán:
> Nora, you lit up my life in ways you will never begin to understand. You saved me from the darkness and in return all I did was to drag you down into this dangerous world. I will never forgive myself

> for what happened to you. I understand you need time and space. I hope and pray that one day you come back to me, but for now just know that I love you and I will always be here if you ever need anything. My réaltín álainn.

The tears I was so desperately holding back begin to flow hard and fast. I wish I could just hate him, but I don't. I'm still so in love with him.

Chapter Fifty-Five

Aodhán

"Get up!" Mac shouts as he kicks the sofa in my office. My eyes shoot open and I grunt in his direction. I'd been sleeping here since the day I cleared all her things out of the house. It felt even more empty now than it had before I met her. It was just a house before. Now she's gone, it feels more like an empty vacuum. I can't stand to be there.

"Bro, you gotta get your shite together, you can't keep doing this?"

My head is thumping and my eyes are like two piss holes in the snow. That will be the whiskey from last night. "I can't go back there, not without her."

"Well, that may be, but we have business to attend to. Murphy called, he has a proposition he wants to put to us and said he's bringing a sweetener."

"Why the fuck would we accept anything from him?"

"He said it is linked to Nora. Let's hear him out at least."

SEEN

I jump up from the couch and my hands ball into fists. "If he had anything to do with this, I'll kill him on site, fuck the consequences.'

"Let's just see what he has to say first. Come on, you'll need coffee. He's going to be here in 20 minutes."

Murphy arrives with his top guys which surprises me. This must be serious if the whole leadership is here. Mac is leading the discussion from our side, while I am struggling to contain my anger. The man in front of us had been the bane of our lives for years. My father never spoke of what their beef was, only that it went back to when they were teenagers.

At over six feet tall, he could tower over most men, but I refuse to be intimidated by him. His dark hair has begun to show signs of greying, hardly surprising given his age, but the beard he is now sporting is most definitely more grey than black. He reminds me of George Clooney, and has the cocky attitude to boot.

I can't even bring myself to shake the man's hand, the ultimate show of disrespect in our world, and yet, he laughs it off. "Nevermind kid, you'll be thanking me shortly."

"Doubt it. Why don't you just get to why you are here so the rest of us can get on with our day."

"I was sorry to hear about your girl, Nora, isn't it?"

"Don't you dare say her name," I sneer. My blood boils at the mere mention of her from his lips.

"Aodh, watch it," Mac snaps at me. "Listen, Murphy, just spit out whatever you came here to say."

"Ok, fine. There is a new organisation in town and they are encroaching on both our territories. It's bad for business, and what's worse, they're operating out of a base down at the harbour. They've hit our shipments on more than one occasion."

"I fail to see how that's our problem," Mac sneers while shrugging his shoulders.

"Sure, I guess what is bad for me can only be good for you, right? No, what will interest you though, is that they were responsible for the shooting here. Word on the street is, they want to take over the whole of Belfast. Run the drug trade, and they also specialise in girls."

"Girls?" Mac is fuming. "What the fuck do you mean girls?"

Murphy shakes his head. "They traffic them in. Fill them full of drugs and then pimp them out to the highest bidders. It's fucking disgusting."

"And what exactly do you want from us?" I question, still not really seeing the relevance of his visit, other than pointing me in the direction of my next list of victims.

"If we combine our forces, we could wipe them out and save a lot of women in the process. We would, of course, need to agree to some sort of truce. Let bygones be bygones and all that."

Mac speaks before I can. "And why, exactly, would we trust you enough to agree to that?"

"Ah yes, I forgot my sweetener." He motions to his men who drag in two hooded figures and throw them at our feet. They lie there squirming with their ankles bound by ropes and wrists cable-tied behind their backs. The henchmen pick them both up and rip off the hoods.

The older man I was unfamiliar with stood with his face bruised and bleeding. The younger of them was all too familiar to me. The little scumbag we picked up a few weeks back. The one responsible for setting me up for the robbery.

A flash of recognition crosses the older man's eyes as he looks between Mac and I, but it is the fear in the younger man's face that intrigues me. He remembers my threat from last time. He begins to twist and squirm harder, attempting to free himself from the tight grip holding him secure.

"What the fuck is this?" I ask, still not putting the pieces together of what is happening here.

"Ah, well, I know you are aware of young Francis here. He didn't take too kindly to your treatment of him recently and tried to enlist my help in retaliation. When I refused he, and his father here, jumped ship, and have been feeding information to the new crew about both our organisations. Oh, and did I forget to mention, these two like to ride motorcycles at night time." The last sentence comes with a wink and all of a sudden it clicks into place.

They were responsible for the shooting.

Mac holds his arm across my chest attempting to keep me back. "Wait, how can we trust this?"

Murphy interjects, "I don't want a war with you. We need to stop this new crew. We can't allow them to come in and take everything we have worked for off us. I don't have the manpower to deal with these guys on my own. Divided we both fall, but together we win."

It sounds like sense, but I don't want to trust him. I already know Mac was considering it from the moment Murphy mentioned the trafficking of women. Mac could gut and kill like the best of us, but the mistreatment of women triggered something in him like nothing else ever could.

Mac turns to me and I can see it in his eyes, the truth of what I already know. He didn't even need to say it. He wants this truce, he wants to take down that organisation. I don't care about either of those things.

"You do you, but I want those two. No questions asked."

Mac nods. "Of course, but one more thing. This war is mine. Take care of these two, then concentrate on this place, and getting her back. No questions asked."

I can't help but laugh at his repetition of my own words. The rest was an order, one I wanted to fight against, but knew that it was pointless. Once Mac made up his mind there was no going back. I'm not able to say the words, so I just nod.

"Murphy, you've got your truce. Thanks for bringing them to us. We will take care of it from here."

"Wise choice, Mac. You know, your father would be proud of you. We'll be in touch." With that they leave. The henchmen drop little Francis and his father to the ground on their way out.

Chapter Fifty-Six

Nora

Waking up on my first morning back at my apartment, was the first time, I felt this alone in a long time. As I motion to move, I feel a weight on my legs. Looking down, I spot Sooty and Ghost curled up on top of the duvet. That's odd. They've never been the type of cats to sleep on my bed.

I lean forward to pet them. I missed the soft feel of their fur. They both stretch out, then proceed to pop off the bed and sit by the door.

I pull myself together and make my way into the bathroom. I turn on the shower and make sure the temperature is just right before stepping in. The water cascades over my body and it reminds me of the morning before the shooting. I huff and shake my head at how frustrated he left me. No matter what I do, he penetrates my thoughts.

I try to distract myself by washing my hair, but it hurts to raise my arms above my head. One hand wash will have to do. My fingers then trace along my surgery line.

The bigger stitches came out before I left the hospital, and while the dissolvable ones are starting to fade, the wound is still red and swollen, although healing. I imagine it will be quite a scar once it's fully healed.

The wound on my arm where the bullet went straight through is less painful, or perhaps it only feels that way because the one on my stomach hurts so much.

Opting for baggy track bottoms and my favourite hoodie, I finally get dressed and make myself coffee and toast before curling up in my egg chair. Perhaps a little on the nose given everything that has happened recently, but I find myself choosing a mafia romance–Orlov: Shadows of Pine Hill by Ava Rouge and Raven Emberwolf–as my next read.

The next few hours whiz pass in a flash and as I close the book, I start to draw similarities to the female main character and her stubbornness. I wanted to scream at her for giving her man such a hard time. Maybe I'm being too hard on Aodhán.

I lose myself in that thought until I hear a knock at the door. When I open the door, there is no one there. However, on the mat there is a brown takeaway bag. Peering inside I see a soup container and a sandwich. I can already smell the soup–chicken noodle, my favourite.

Throwing caution to the wind, I bring it inside and open it up. I didn't even realise I was hungry until the smells hit me. Unwrapping the sandwich, I notice the thick gammon slices and yellow english mustard stacked between two thick cut pieces of Belfast Bap.

Sitting at the table to eat, I reach for my phone and message the girls.

> **Me:**
> Please tell me one of you sent me lunch?

> **Jenna:**
> What? Nope wasn't me.

> **Emily:**
> Nor me. OMG what did he send you?

> **Me:**
> I was hoping it was one of you. Chicken noodle soup with a ham and mustard Belfast Bap.

> **Jenna:**
> Have you still not contacted him?

> **Me:**
> No, I don't know that I'm ready to talk to him. I don't even know what I would say.

> **Emily:**
> It might be a wild idea and totally out there but what about simply "Thanks for lunch"

> **Jenna:**
> It would certainly be a start. There is nothing to say you have to engage beyond that if you don't want to.

> **Me:**
> I guess.

I set the phone down and finish up the food. Can I really just do that? Will he expect more? Am I ready for that? I wish I knew what to do for the best. What if I can't move beyond this? Would texting him be cruel if I can't?

I do miss him and I do love him. Is it enough to start there?

Chapter Fifty-Seven

Aodhán

Staring at these two pieces of shite lying on the floor of the club, the thoughts race through my head of all the ways I could torture them. All the ways I could make them pay for daring to hurt her. To hurt what was mine.

I rip the duck tape off the old man's mouth. I want him to beg for his life and that of his son. I want to hear their pathetic excuses before I kill them. He just looks at me. I see the cogs turning in his head, like he knows what I want and has decided nothing he says will change what is so obviously going to happen.

I pick up his son and he screams, "Wait... just wait it was me, he was just driving the bike. You have me, I'm the one you really want. Please, just let him go."

That makes me laugh. Neither of them are walking away from this. "Let him go? Not a chance." I pull out my gun and shoot the kid in the head, like I should have done the last time we picked him up. The old man stills, staring down at his son, laid out on the ground, blood pooling around his body, just like hers did that night.

My phone buzzes and I take a moment to check it. It's a message from her. My heart leaps. This is the first time she has reached out. I knew she was released yesterday and the girls had taken her back to the apartment. Knowing her, I was concerned she wouldn't take care of herself, so I'd organised her favourite lunch to be delivered.

Sure enough it would have arrived by now. Opening the message that I'd been desperately hoping for. I see only two words.

> Nora:
> Thank you

Short and simple and yet it feels like hope. Like her, it's a shining ray of light in this vast darkness I've been struggling in for weeks.

It instantly lifts my mood and I'm no longer driven by the need to make this man suffer any further. He just watched his son die and he's next. The thought of torturing him no longer brings me any delight, nor do I want to waste anymore time on him. I turn and aim the gun at him. He doesn't even look up as I pull the trigger.

Mac places his hand on my shoulder. "You good man? Not like you to make it painless, especially given this situation."

SEEN

"It's Nora, she... she reached out, Mac. I mean it's only a thank you but she made contact. It's... it's... it's gotta be a good thing, right?"

His hand grips me harder as he pulls me in for a hug. "Yeah, Aodh, I think it could be a good thing. Just don't rush her, ok?"

"I know, I know. I won't. Well, I'll try not to."

He laughs and steps back. He motions to the guys behind us. "Fellas, make sure this gets cleaned up, we are open in a few hours. Can't have blood stains on the ground as our guests arrive"

I look back at her message. It takes all my restraint not to call her straight away. Instead, I opt for a simple reply.

> **Me:**
> I hope you enjoy it. Remember, anything you need, I'm here.

She leaves it on read for a few minutes, and then her reply appears.

> **Nora:**
> *smiling emoji*

It may not be an open door, but it's a start, and I can work with that. It's time to get my girl back.

Flicking through my contacts, I call the one person I need on side for this to work. It feels like forever waiting for the call to be answered, and when it is, I'm not entirely surprised by the greeting.

"Are you calling to arrange your funeral, asshole?"

She is not going to make this easy. "Good afternoon to you too, Emily, always a pleasure. Listen, I know I fucked up but I really need your help."

"My help? Why exactly would I want to help you?"

I outline my plan, answering every question she throws my way. So far, she's not said no. The line goes silent.

"You still there?"

"Yes, I'm still here. I'm thinking."

A few minutes pass and I'm desperate to ask again, but I can't afford to piss her off any further. Finally, she speaks.

"Fine. I'll help, but if this backfires, I swear some rival gang will be the least of your worries."

"I got it, and Emily, thank you. I really appreciate this."

"Yeah, you better!" And with that she disconnects the call.

Time to put the rest of the plan in motion now. Time to take back what is mine.

Chapter Fifty-Eight

Nora

I'd kept my head down for the last week, recuperating and vegetating in the sea of new books. Work has been amazing. Obviously I haven't told them I was shot. That would have raised some serious red flags in my security clearance.

No, the cover story of appendicitis worked well, seeing as it was something that could be explained by the sudden need for surgery and the recovery time I required. Although, I did hate lying to them. Mel has been good to me.

Looking up from my book, the banging on the door sounded like the peelers have arrived with a SWAT team, but alas, I knew it was the girls arriving. They'd messaged earlier begging for a night out. Of course I said no, and then they said they were coming over anyway. I love those girls.

Emily bounces in through the door before I can even properly open it. "We have something super cool planned, and it's time to get you dressed cause, we're going out, bitch!"

It's always been hard to say no to her. She's always the one picking us up and keeping us going. If she says it's super cool, then I know I'm going to enjoy it. She's never wrong about these things.

Even though I am able to move more freely, Jenna insists on doing my hair while Emily flicks through the clothes hanging in my wardrobe before settling on a sleek, long sleeved black and silver maxi dress.

"Girl, you look smoking hot in that dress," Emily squeals as I step out into the living room after getting dressed.

"One final touch," Jenna states as she slips a blindfold over my eyes.

"What's with the blindfold, girls?"

"We told you, it's a surprise," Emily laughs as she guides me out of the apartment and to the car

"No peeking, or Emily will kick your ass, and recovery or not, I'll let her," Jenna whispers.

It feels like we have been driving forever when the car finally comes to a stop and I hear the doors open. Jenna walks me forward and instructs me when to step. A familiar smell starts to invade my senses, one I know I should recognise, but can't quite put my finger on it.

One minute they are holding me, and the next they step away. I turn, even though I can't see anything. "Emily? Jenna?"

When they don't answer, I reach up to remove the blindfold. I realise exactly where I am. I am standing in the entrance hall of Shadows facing the front door, and neither of my supposed best friends, are anywhere to be seen. The whole place is dead, which is strange for a Saturday night.

The thought crosses my mind to just leave. I could so easily do it, just walk out the front door, but they dropped me here for a reason and I want to know what it is.

Deep breaths, Nora, you can do this. I keep whispering it to myself like a silent prayer as I turn and walk further into the club. My eyes dart all round until they focus in on the man standing on the dancefloor.

All six feet of him, standing tall, in a dark blue suit that clings to his body, his muscles, like a second skin. He wrings his hands like a nervous tick and his face betrays the worry beneath the confidence he normally tries to exude. My breath catches in my throat.

I look back towards the door. "Nora..." It's raw and like a cry of pain. "Please don't leave. Just give me five minutes, and then, if you still want to leave, I won't stand in your way."

I turn back towards him and nod. Not trusting myself enough to speak right now. He walks towards me, and steps right in front of me. My body tenses, I could so easily reach out and touch him if I wanted to. I do want to, but I also want to hear what he has to say.

"From the very first moment I saw you in that car park, I was mesmerised by you. Your beauty, your confidence, it was shining out of you like the brightest light I've ever encountered. I just knew that I had to find you, know you."

He takes my hands in his as he continues, "I know it was unconventional, but I needed to be close to you, and then when we were together, I swear it's the happiest I've ever been. Losing you was the worst thing that ever happened to me. I love you, réaltín álainn. You light up my life and bring so much joy and love into my life. I feel like I can't breathe without you."

He steps back slightly, tears glistening in his eyes. "I can't see my life without you by my side. I will spend the rest of my life protecting you, loving you, and trying to be the best man for you. I want to make you as happy as you make me."

The lump in my throat threatens to choke me while the tears well in my eyes. It's overwhelming when he drops to one knee. Still holding both my hands in one of his, he reaches into his pocket and pulls out a little blue box.

"Nora, I love you more than life itself. Please say you will be my wife?"

Chapter Fifty-Nine

Aodhán

Time stands still as I search her face for some hint of what she is thinking or feeling, but she is just staring at me. Her face is completely unreadable. She motions for me to stand. My heart begins to shatter.

"Aodhán, I...."

Fuck! I drop my head to my chest. I don't think I can watch her leaving.

"Aodhán, I love you too..." My head snaps up, and I look into her eyes as I reach for her. She holds up her hand. "I'm not finished. I love you so much, I was terrified of how much. It was suffocating to think that something could happen to you, so I pushed you away to protect us both. But seeing you here, and hearing you say you love me, I couldn't walk away now if I tried. So yes, yes, I'll marry you, you bloody stalker." She bites her bottom lip holding in a laugh.

I let out the breath I didn't even realise I was holding and pick her up, spinning her around. I gently set her back down on the floor, and cupping her face my lips find hers effortlessly, as I consume her like she is the very air I need to breathe.

We pour all our emotions into that kiss, all the missed time together, all the desire we both clearly have for each other. Breaking contact ever so slightly, I whisper, "Come with me."

She nods as I take her hand and lead her to my office. She pulls on my hand as we reach the door, "I really missed you, Aodhán,"

"Oh baby, I'm about to show you just how much I missed you. Don't think for one second, I don't know that you've been touching yourself and calling out my name. I'm going to worship your body and fuck you so hard that all you remember is my name."

I set her on the edge of my desk and run my hands up her legs. One hand grips her underwear and I tear it off, while the other holds her throat with just enough pressure to secure her in place.

I slip my fingers inside her, the warmth and wetness of her pussy enveloping me. I kiss her soft lips as she moans and begins to grind on my fingers. I drive them further in while my thumb circles her clit. Her pussy starts to pulse as her orgasm builds and I whip my fingers out. She huffs and I laugh.

"Don't worry, I'm just getting started." I pull the dress up and over her head so she is naked on my desk wearing only her heels. I step forward and cage her in, devouring her lips and peppering kisses along her jaw, down her neck, moving to suck a nipple into my mouth. Sucking on it gently, I nibble just a little while I tease the other with my fingers.

Her moans are like a drug I'm addicted to and can't get enough of. I release her nipples and continue to kiss down her body. I hover over her scar, taking care to trace it ever so carefully with my lips.

Falling to my knees, I lift one leg up over my shoulder and I dive into that sweet, warm and wet pussy I've been dreaming about for days. Fuck, I have missed this. I've missed her. My tongue alternates from licking her clit to fucking her pussy. That familiar feeling of her tensing around it makes me drive it in further as she crashes over the edge of her orgasm and rides my face all the way through it.

I lick her clean as she lays down on the desk to catch her breath. Standing, I remove my trousers and boxers. I fist my hard rock cock as I lift her to face me. Reaching up, I cup her face once again and crash into her lips. She licks my tongue and moans, tasting herself on me. That action alone almost makes me cum.

I pick her up and she wraps her legs around my waist. Gripping her ass, I walk towards my chair and sit. She hovers on my lap, pinching my chin. "Fuck me, Aodhán, I want to feel every inch of you."

I thrust my cock into her and she gasps. I don't give her time to adjust as I slam in and out of her, one hand holding the back of her neck, the other digging into her ass cheek. Her hair falls over her face as she chases another release. I pull her head back so I can stare into her eyes. "I want to watch you unravel on my cock, baby. Milk it for all it's worth."

She cums hard, coating me in her juices and her pussy has my cock in a vice like grip as I continue to thrust. She bites down on my neck, not quite breaking the skin and my own release roars out of me as I cum harder than I've done in my life.

She collapses into me, and I wrap my arms around her body. I don't want to ever let go.

Chapter Sixty

Nora

I'm not sure how long we just sit there, basking in the glow of our epic fuck session. Who knew makeup sex could be so hot? I'm pretty sure my legs have turned to jelly. I shift my head slightly, nuzzling further into the groove of his neck, as he tightens his hold on me.

I feel his fingers brush the hair back from my face, and I open my eyes. He shifts me in his lap releasing himself from inside me. His eyes focus on me with an intensity I don't think I've seen before. "D... Did you really say yes? Tell me, I didn't just dream it."

It's then that I understand the look. It is one of total vulnerability as I watch this big strong man's eyes roam up and down my face, desperate for an answer, and it makes me love him all the harder. "You didn't dream it, Aodhán. I'm your fiancée and you are stuck with me now."

His pupils dilate as he stares lovingly into mine. Those beautiful lips pull upwards as he flashes the widest grin I've ever seen splashed across his face. "I love the sound of that. There is only one thing that sounds better."

"Oh yeah, and what's that?"

He gently lowers my forehead onto his and closes his eyes. "When I get to call you my wife."

"Well then, what are we waiting for, *husband* to be."

His hand slips behind my head and he crushes my lips in a bruising kiss, while I feel him begin to harden beneath me.

He lifts me and sets me ever so gently on the edge of the desk, before helping me back into my dress. Lifting his trousers, the little box falls from his pocket. The sound of laughter fills the room as he drops down to one knee again. "I guess in all my haste, I never actually got this on your finger. I better do it quickly, before you change your mind"

He opens the box and nestled inside is the most beautiful ring. A white gold band with a circular sapphire jewel surrounded by smaller diamonds. It is the most beautiful thing I have ever seen. He slides it on to my finger and it fits perfectly, like it was made just for me.

"Aodhán, it is stunning."

"It pales in comparison to your beauty, but I must say you are stunning in it. Now come on, let's get out of here or you'll end up bent back over that desk in only the ring."

He may be laughing, but the cheeky twinkle in his eye tells me he's deadly serious, and while the idea is something I would certainly be up for, I think we could both do with sustenance.

Walking up the stairs and into the bar area, we are greeted by my girls, Mac and Riley. An intense heat flashes across my face as my cheeks burn with embarrassment, the smirks on their faces telling me they already know exactly where, and–oh my god–what we were doing. I raise my hands to shield my face and the girls rush me, almost knocking me over as they throw their arms around me in a vice grip hug while squealing.

Emily is the first to speak. "Didn't I promise you'd enjoy your surprise?" She grins like a Cheshire cat, confirming what I already thought–Aodhán got to her. He couldn't have pulled this off without her.

She's a tough cookie, and I would have loved to have been a fly on the wall for that conversation. No way she gave him an easy time. These girls have always had my back and I would be completely lost without them. They are definitely the type of friends every girl should have in her corner.

Jenna lifts my hand to inspect the ring. "Holy sweet fuck, the boy did good. And you look like you celebrated hard." She laughs as she fixes the back of my hair.

The initial embarrassment eases and I find the humour in the situation. It's not like I wouldn't have told them everything anyway. I just didn't think it would be so soon. "Well, I wasn't exactly expecting a welcoming party afterwards."

"Girl, now you know fine rightly, we weren't leaving until we knew you were ok, one way or another. Oh, and by the way, it's a bloody good job, those boys made those offices soundproof."

"Emily, don't embarrass her any further."

"It's ok, Jenna, it was pretty fucking epic." They join me in a fit of giggles as we huddle close together enjoying our champagne.

Chapter Sixty-One

Aodhán

As the girls pull Nora into a group hug, I step off to the side and make my way to the bar. Mac is first up to congratulate me. I couldn't have done any of this without his help. He's had a rough couple of weeks following the truce negotiations with Murphy and the investigation of the underground group.

Mac drags me in towards him and grips me a bear hug. "I'm so glad you two finally sorted things out."

"Yeah, dude, your moping about was getting real old," Riley laughs as he taps me on the shoulder, wrestling me out of Mac's arms before lifting me into the air and spinning me around like a kid. He's always been the joker of the three of us. We managed to keep him somewhat out of our illegal business, so he's not tormented like us.

"Jeez, wee man, come on. Put me down before you drop me on my head." He sets me down with thud.

Once I regain my composure, Mac hands me a glass of champagne. "Don't worry the bubbles are just for a toast, the whiskey is already poured. Nora, I'm not exactly sure what it is you see in this big lug right here," he places his hand on my shoulder, "but I am so delighted to officially welcome you to the family. To Aodhán and Nora."

"To Aodhán and Nora." Echoes around the room as she slips into my arms and kisses me.

Watching Nora laugh and celebrate with her friends, as I did the same with my brothers, felt like our very own fairytale tale ending. I certainly never imagined being here like this the morning I woke up in the cells. It's funny how life works out and just when you least expect it, it throws you a curveball you just never saw coming.

Chapter Sixty-Two

Nora

Epilogue

Bouncing out of bed in a blind panic, I rush to throw on clothing and race to the kitchen, leaving Aodhán still snoring his pretty little head off. As things became more intense over the last few months with Cormac's work, I offered to take over the traditional sunday dinner duties. It always goes great, but today I have a surprise for the boys.

While clearing out the attic recently to get some space to store some of my things, I came across a box of their mother's things. One of which was her recipe book. Having studied it for ages, I've decided to make one of her dessert recipes for them.

It's terrifying, and a little exciting, all at the same time. Retrieving the box of ingredients from the boot of my car where they've been hiding since yesterday, I can't help but smile at how different things are now from six months ago.

I never imagined being this happy, this in love, with a man who absolutely worships the ground I walk on. Slicing up the apples and plums, careful to ensure they are similarly sized for equal cooking is the easy part. I layer them into the base of the dish, before mixing the remaining items together in a bowl and pouring over the top. I finish off the dish with a generous dusting of brown sugar and then place in the oven to bake.

With the all important surprise dish in the oven, I start prepping the rest of the meal, just as Aodhán joins me. His arms wrap around my waist while he nudges my hair off my shoulder and kisses my neck. It sends tingles down my body, and I lean backwards into his, releasing a soft moan. "Aodhán, I'm trying to make dinner. The guys will be here soon."

"You left me alone in our bed, do you honestly think you could get away with that?" His voice low and growling as his hands roam my body, one hand under my shirt, fingers twirling around my nipple, the other down my trousers rubbing my clit and teasing my pussy. "Always so wet and ready for me, réaltín álainn."

His hot breath on my neck continues to tingle as he pushes two fingers inside me and begins to massage my clit. "Ah... Aodhán, more." He adds a third as he finger fucks me across the counter. The sensations paired with the pinching of my nipple and his mouth on my neck, have me panting hard, chasing my release.

He doesn't let up for a second as I hurtle towards the edge of the abyss and when his teeth clamp down on my neck, my body shudders and floods with intense pleasure. He holds me in place as the wave continues to wash over me, only withdrawing his hand when it completely abates.

I attempt to steady myself on the counter once he steps back. The slurping noise from behind has me spinning on my toes. I watch him lick his fingers clean all while he grins and maintains direct eye contact. "Mmh, you taste so sweet, I could die with this delicious flavour on my tongue."

I pull my bottom lip between my teeth as he steps forward. His lips crush into mine, and I can taste myself on his tongue as he slides it so effortless into my mouth. I will never be able to get enough of this glorious man.

"As much as I would love to do this all day long, I'm going to grab a quick shower and then I'll be back to help."

I whimper as he pulls back from me and heads towards the door. His laughter echoes through the house.

As I add the final touches to our meal, voices boom from the front hall. Riley bounces into the kitchen like a duracell powered tigger, lifting me in his strong arms and hugging me so tight, I swear he's going to crush me. I wish I could bottle his energy and sell it, I'd make a fortune. Cormac walks in behind Aodhán, the stress and horrors of the past few months plastered across his face. It saddens me to think about what he's dealing with, and his refusal to allow any of us in has been the hardest thing to accept. I'm hoping my little surprise will lift his spirits.

"You guys get settled in the dining room, food will be served momentarily."

We settle into our usual comfortable routine over dinner as everyone but Cormac chats about what's going on. He remains stoic at the end of the table, always listening but never divulging details.

My stomach begins doing somersaults as the boys finish their food, knowing that dessert is imminent. What if they hate it, or worse hate the fact that I made it?

Excusing myself, I rush into the kitchen, needing a moment to settle the racing in my chest. Lifting the tray out of the oven, I set it on the counter, when thoughts of earlier flood my brain and a sense of peace washes over me.

Picking up the dessert, I take a deep breath and head back to the dining room. "Dessert is served. I... I hope you like it." My voice is slightly shaky, not so much that Riley and Cormac notice but Aodhán is by my side in an instant.

"Nora, are you ok?" His words are laced with concern.

"Yes, of course. I'm just a little nervous." His brows furrow as I motion for him to sit. I begin dishing the pudding into bowls and passing them to the boys.

Within the first few bites, all three are staring at me, then looking between themselves. My heart is beating so fast, I begin to feel faint until Cormac speaks.

"This is incredible, it tastes just like..." The words are lost on the tip of his tongue, he can only look between the dish and me.

"Like mum's." Riley completes the thought.

They all look toward me with curiosity. "I found her recipe book a few days ago, and thought I'd try to make it. The page was the most worn in the book, so I figured it must have been one of her favourites. I hope you don't mind."

Aodhán pulls my chair closer to him. With two fingers under my chin, he forces me to look at him. "Mind? Nora, of course we don't mind. Is this what you've been stressing about all day?"

"I... I just didn't want to offend you all. I just wanted to do something nice."

"This is perfect, baby. She would have loved you, you know," he declares, pulling me into his warm embrace. I will never tire of this man and how much he loves me.

Molly B's Rice Pudding

Ingredients:
- 2 cups of full fat milk
- 1 cup of pudding rice
- Knob of butter
- Large handful of dried fruit
- 2 tablespoons of brown sugar

Instructions:
1. Mix the ingredients together and pour into an oven proof dish
2. Bake in the oven for 1 hour until rice is soft and brown crust forms on top

Once cooked sprinkle brown sugar on top to form a sugar crust. (For Cormac)

Add a layer of thinly sliced cooking apples before pouring the mix. (For Aodhán)

Add thinly slice plums, alternating with the apple slices. (For Riley)

Glossary

This book contains local colloquialisms for Belfast and/or Northern Ireland where it is set.

Scundered - In Belfast this means embarrassed and not bored or tired as my hockey wife would tell you :)

Dander - We don't simply walk or go for a stroll. We go for a dander.

Hoke - A rummage, poking around.

Mucker - a friend, a mate.

Réaltín Álainn - Beautiful little star

Acknowledgements

I still can't believe I wrote a book.

The idea for this series came to me on my way to work one morning last spring. Standing outside the courthouse as a prison transport van passed me. I noticed the blacked out windows and wondered if the person inside could see out.

That thought began to build and Aodhán's story was born. From there, the idea grew to include his brothers Cormac and Riley, who will have their own adventures later in the series.

I want to thank my little Claire Bear who was with me every step of the way through this journey. I spent countless hours melting her head about ideas and story threads but without her feedback and encouragement this would not have been possible.

To my alpha and beta readers who helped me shape this tale. Thank you for taking time out of your busy lives to read my story and offer your advice and guidance it means the world to me.

Thank you to my wonderful cover designer Juniper who I have absolutely tortured and yet she couldn't do enough to help and support me.

To my awesome editor Jasmine who took my story and made it incredible. I can never thank you enough for your help, guidance and support. Without you this book would not be the beautiful piece of art it is. You took my vision and made it a reality.

To Mark and Mynx thank you for your amazing photographs and artistry.

To my long suffering husband Patrick who has endured so many hours of me harping on about this book and this journey. Thank you for always being in my corner. I love you.

Finally to you, lovely reader, I am grateful for your support and I hope you have enjoyed this book as much as I've enjoyed creating it.

Until next time.

Shauna x

About the author

Shauna Adams is an Irish Romance author who lives in Belfast with her husband, two children and three cats. On the nights she isn't cheering on the Belfast Giants Ice Hockey team, she loves nothing more than curling up with a mug of coffee and a good book - dark romance, Rom-Coms or romantasy as long as they are hot and spicy :)

You can find and follow Shauna on her social medias here: https://linktr.ee/srafams

Printed in Great Britain
by Amazon